Still a
Work in
Progress

Still a Work in Progress

Jo Knowles

CANDLEWICK PRESS

First edition 2016

Library of Congress Catalog Card Number pending
ISBN 978-0-7636-7217-1

16 17 18 19 20 21 BVG 10 9 8 7 6 5 4 3 2 1

Printed in Berryville, VA, U.S.A.

This book was typeset in Sabon.

Candlewick Press
99 Dover Street
Somerville, Massachusetts 02144

visit us at www.candlewick.com

For Eli: Without you,
this book wouldn't be.

And to the Hartland, VT
carpool riders: Thank you
for the endless supply of
inspiration, laughs, and hope.
You do friendship right.

1

Please Stop Standing on the Toilet Seats

"I am not afraid of Molly Lo," Ryan tells me from inside the stall in the boys' bathroom. He refuses to use the urinal, just like everyone else.

"Then why are you hiding in the bathroom?" I ask.

"She's stalking me," he says. "Stalkers make me nervous."

The toilet does not flush as Ryan's head appears at the top of the wobbly metal wall of the stall . . . then his sneaker, as he slings his leg over. He struggles with getting all the way over, grunting and cursing, then finally slides down the side to land in front of me.

"You forgot to flush," I point out.

He shrugs and straightens his shirt. "I'm conserving water. 'If it's yellow, let it mellow.'"

"Seriously? No wonder it smells so bad in here."

I wait for him to wash his hands.

No one knows who the original person was to leave the door to the stall locked from the inside, but for some reason, no one wants to be the person to unlock it. This means that in order to use the bathroom, you have to either crawl under or climb over to get in and out. Since crawling under would mean having to touch the boys'-room floor with your hands, there's really only one choice.

I usually just try to hold it.

"I wish she'd get the hint that I'm not interested," Ryan says. He peers into the mirror to inspect a zit on his upper lip.

"You should pop that and get it over with," I tell him.

"I know, but I bit my fingernails down too far and can't get a good squeeze." He gives me a look as if he's considering asking me to do it for him.

I give him a *Not a chance* look back.

"Forget it," he says. "Just c'mon." The mini volcano on his upper lip leads us out.

In the hallway, Lily Smith is standing next to Small Tyler and pointing at his locker. "We know it's you," she says, all bossy. "And it's disgusting. You have to clean it out."

"It *is* clean," Small Tyler tells her. Small Tyler isn't actually that small, but the other Tyler in school, Tyler Gingritch, is kind of a giant, and that's how people distinguish the two of them.

"What smells like fish?" Belle asks, coming up behind Lily. She wrinkles her nose and whips her long, shiny black braids over her shoulder at the same time. Belle is an eighth-grader, but she's friends with Lily because Lily *acts* like an eighth-grader.

"What's the problem out here?" We all turn to see the Tank coming down the hallway. His actual name is Mr. Sticht and he teaches social studies. All the girls love the Tank. He has huge muscles and a tattoo on his arm of some military crest that everyone in his unit got when they were deployed in Iraq. The Tank is our hero, even though most of us are from families who opposed the war. I think you can be antiwar but still be grateful to people who have to go fight in one. No one messes with the Tank, and no one *ever* calls him that to his face.

The small crowd moves aside as he approaches the locker, which, now that people have cleared a path, does smell suspiciously like fish.

The Tank swings open the locker, and a wave of even stronger fishiness wafts over us. People cough and gag.

Small Tyler steps back. "I swear there's nothing in there," he says. "I've looked! It's just paper and stuff."

The Tank steps backward. "Well something's making that smell," he says, covering his face with his enormous hand.

"Maybe someone put something in there as a joke," Small Tyler suggests.

"It smells like death," Ryan says.

Someone laughs.

"OK, OK, pull everything outta there," the Tank orders. "Someone go get the trash can."

Max Fitzsimmons volunteers, holding his arms out as he struts down the hall, as if his muscles are so big they prevent his arms from resting at his sides.

Ryan elbows me and rolls his eyes. "His muscles aren't *that* big," he mutters, shaking his head in disgust.

"Whose muscles aren't that big?" our friend Sam asks way too loudly, coming to stand between us.

"Tell you later," Ryan says.

Max drags the trash barrel back, and everyone steps even farther away because the trash smells *almost* as bad as Small Tyler's locker.

"Well, get going," the Tank tells Small Tyler.

He starts pulling crumpled papers, books, and other stuff out of his locker.

"How did you accumulate so much junk in just two months?" the Tank asks.

Small Tyler shrugs. The tips of his ears are bright red. I feel bad that we're all just standing around watching him. We're not *good* friends, but I do like the guy. Our school is on the small side, so everyone is kind of friends at some level.

I step forward and motion for Small Tyler to hand me the trash from his locker so he doesn't have to do it all by himself.

"Thanks, Noah," he mumbles.

The more he empties it out, though, the stronger the smell. People step back farther and farther down the hall. Even the Tank looks a little worried about what we're going to find when we get to the bottom.

I glance over at Ryan and Sam, who have stepped way back from the scene, shaking their heads at me, as if I'm the biggest sucker in the world.

This is what I get for being the nice guy.

Small Tyler stops. "Uhhhhh," he says quietly.

"What is it?" I ask.

A few people step closer, risking the smell just to see. People have a sick fascination with gross things.

Slowly Small Tyler lifts another handful of crumpled-up balls of paper out of his locker, but these ones have something brownish dripping from them. He tries to hand them to me, but I step back. Even *I* have my limits.

Unfortunately I'm not fast enough, and a drip lands on my sneaker.

"What. Is. *That?*" the Tank asks, screwing up his face.

"Locker juice," someone whispers.

"Ewwwww," everyone whispers back.

"Well, get it the hell out of there!" the Tank bellows. He drags the trash barrel closer so Small Tyler can get the dripping trash in without getting any on the floor — or anyone else's shoes.

When he tosses it in, an even stronger smell hits me all at once, and I stagger backward into Max, who staggers into Lily. We are like dominoes falling into one another and gasping, eyes watering. I try to think of a worse smell but can't, and that's saying something. There are three things I can think of off the top of my head. A dead mouse whose smell spread through the whole school the day the heat kicked in for the first time this fall. Tyler Gingritch's farts after his parents had a chili-contest party in October and he wandered through the school leaving gas in every room just to torture us all, and then Zach Bray and Max Fitzsimmons, who were also at the party, formed a group called the Fart Squad and went around leaving stink bombs right before class. And finally Mrs. Phelps's coffee breath, better known as Death Breath. It fills the science room every morning and makes even Miranda-with-the-Always-Stuffed-Up-Nose gag.

This is the smell of a thousand dead mice. A million Fart Squad bombings. And worse than a fan blowing Mrs. Phelps's Death Breath *straight into your mouth.*

"I found it!" Small Tyler says, holding up a leaky sandwich bag. It looks like it once held a sandwich but now holds a brown, moldy thing with putrid liquid dripping out.

"Tuna sandwich," he says. Then he covers his mouth with his hand like he's trying not to throw up.

Students start gagging and stumbling down the hall. The Tank points to the garbage can and yells, "Drop it in! Drop it in!" as if he's yelling to one of his commando buddies during mortal combat to drop a grenade down an enemy's trench.

Tears roll down Small Tyler's face. It's not clear if they're from humiliation or the horrible odor. It doesn't matter. We all understand.

He quickly drops the dripping bag into the trash. Then, in one brave gesture, he scoops up all the remaining dripping papers at the bottom of his locker in his arms and dumps them in. The Tank slams down the rubber lid and motions to Max, who grabs the handle and quickly wheels the garbage down the hall.

"Take it out! All the way out!" the Tank hollers. Everyone jumps out of the way as Max wheels the trash and the stench to the front door of the school.

"You know where the cleaning supplies are," the

Tank says to Small Tyler, wiping his eyes. "Everyone else, Community Meeting!"

Small Tyler heads to the janitor's closet while the rest of us walk down the hall to the Community Room. I turn back to see him standing at his open locker with a roll of paper towels and a spray bottle. I feel guilty for leaving him, but not enough to get any closer to that smell.

"Now you know why we keep telling you not to leave food in your locker!" the Tank says as he ushers us down the hall.

Lesson learned.

Community Meeting happens once a week. Everyone in the school has to go, including the teachers. The Community Room used to be the music room, but our town had budget cuts and they cut the music program. The walls are painted green, and old couches donated by various families line the walls so that if we're all sitting on them, we form a circle/square. The problem is that there are more students than seats on the couches, so if you get to Community Meeting late, you're stuck sitting on a beanbag or on the floor in front of the couch sitters. The beanbags are mysteriously sticky and smell like dirty sheets. The floor is cold and kind of gross because it doesn't get washed very much. In either case, you have to sit in front of the people on the couch, which means you are close to their feet, which means, depending on who you end up in front of, you are probably going to have a miserable hour.

I look at my own feet and the locker-juice drip left on my sneaker. It's shiny, and I bet sticky, too. I try to rub it off on the floor. This is another reason no one should sit there.

I find an open spot on the red couch next to Sasha Finnegan. I attempt to smile at her, and she surprises me by smiling back. She's the cutest eighth-grader in the school. She's also dating Max, so her smile is likely meaningless. I let myself have a split-second of hope anyway, then remember the locker juice on my shoe and hope it doesn't smell.

Curly, the school cat, pokes her bald head out from behind the couch next to mine. She's hairless and looks more like a little gremlin than a cat. Ms. Cliff, the principal, thinks having a school pet helps the students feel more calm and less stressed. A few years ago the school had a dog that was supposed to be hypoallergenic because he had hair instead of fur, but while he may have had a calming effect on the students, the students didn't have one on him. He developed something called irritable bowel syndrome, and the parents complained that the students shouldn't have to be cleaning up dog poo as part of their education. The principal insisted the school still needed a pet, so they finally settled on Curly.

It's kind of a mystery how anyone could think that Curly could provide comfort and calm. She looks cold and stressed-out all the time, like she lost her coat and can't find it. It seems like the students are the ones constantly trying to comfort the cat instead of the other way around.

Curly jumps on my lap and turns in careful circles. I pet her so she'll settle down. Her skin reminds me of the stingray I got to pet at the New England Aquarium last year. Smooth, even though it looks like it should feel like sandpaper.

Today, Curly's wearing a neon-green vest. Ms. Cliff, who is the art teacher as well as the principal, has a sewing unit in class, and students always make Curly vests for their projects. She needs them to stay warm. I don't know how Curly feels about them, but she puts up with it.

Ms. Cliff motions for all of us to hurry up and settle down. The Tank brings the Suggestion Box over to the group of teachers all sitting on one couch. There's the Tank, who teaches social studies; Ms. Cliff; Mrs. Phelps, the stinky-breath science teacher; Madame Estelle, who teaches French and math; and Mr. Marshall, who teaches English.

Mrs. Phelps reaches into the box and unfolds a slip of paper. "'Please stop standing on the toilet seats,'" she reads.

She looks up and eyes us all suspiciously.

"Do we think this is referring to the boys' room or the girls' room?" she finally asks.

It drives me a little crazy when teachers say "we" as if all of us are one big unit who think the same thoughts and not individual people.

People answer "Boys'" and "Girls'" at the same time.

Mostly it sounds like all the boys said "Girls'" and all the girls said "Boys'."

The girls' room is like a mystery cave to the boys. All we know is that it smells like twenty kinds of body spray vying for air domination. You literally taste it when you walk by the door.

Poor Jem Thomas got the Bathroom Locker this year. That's the one closest to the bathroom entrance. He says even his sandwiches taste like body spray.

"Why would people be standing on the toilets?" Ms. Cliff asks the group.

I glance over at Ryan, who is sitting on one of the beanbag chairs, trying to look innocent. Curly stands up and turns circles on my lap again, pricking my thighs with her tiny claws. Sometimes I think she senses our tension and gets all tense herself.

Sam raises his hand. "To talk to their neighbor?" he asks innocently.

"Gross!" Lily Smith says.

He blushes. "Just a guess."

"Toilets are for sitting on," Ms. Cliff says, all serious.

"Or standing in front of," Ryan points out.

Everyone cracks up.

"We all know what they are *not* for, is the point," says the Tank. "So whoever is standing on the toilets, for whatever reason, please stop. Some people *do* have to sit on them, Ryan, and there's no telling where you all's shoes have been."

Someone makes a gagging noise.

I peer over my lap to inspect the locker juice on my

shoe. This is just one more reason why my option to never use the school toilets unless death from holding it seems imminent is a sound one.

The Tank reaches in for another suggestion. "'Please stop calling the Suggestion Box the Complaint Box,'" he reads.

"Yes," Ms. Cliff says. "That is an excellent *suggestion*. The more you call it a Complaint Box, the more people will complain. We want ideas for making your experience here better."

I'm pretty sure Ms. Cliff is the one who wrote *that* suggestion.

Curly finally settles back down on my lap while Ms. Cliff reads a bunch more complaints disguised as suggestions. Curly's body is extremely warm. I try to pet her again, but her skin creeps me out too much, so I just kind of tap her gently. She closes her eyes and rests her head on my knee.

"Does anyone have any more comments about this week's suggestions?" Ms. Cliff finally asks.

No one does.

After school, I wait on the steps for my ride. My mom is driving today, and I pray she doesn't hop out of the car and wave to me when she gets here like she did on the first day. After that, whenever I got to school, everyone would do the Mom Wave when they saw me. I'm really glad that got boring after a while.

Harper Lewis jumps down the steps next to me and barely manages to land without falling. He stands and swivels to face me.

"Shotgun," he says, grinning.

I roll my eyes. Like I want to sit in the front next to my mom?

Harper and his brother, Stu, live a few blocks from my house, and our parents take turns driving us to and from school. Hardly anyone takes the bus because it takes so long to get home. We only live about a ten-minute drive from school, but if I took the bus, it would be close to an hour because of the route. My dad says it would be good for us to ride the bus, but some high-school kid got beat up right under the bus driver's nose last year, and now my mom insists on driving.

My mom picks us up, and then we head to the high school to get my sister and Stu. There, we wait in the long carpool line. As usual the students take their sweet time saying good-bye to their friends, as if they will never see them again. Emma has to hug everyone.

I catch Harper looking at her dreamily. Everyone looks at Emma that way.

She finally saunters over to the car and climbs in next to me.

"How was your day, honey?" my mom asks cheerfully.

"Fine," Emma says in the same tone. She reaches over and punches my arm. It's how we say hi to each other. I punch her back.

Harper turns around from the front seat. "Hey, Emma," he says hopefully.

She smiles. "Hey, Harper. Nice hat."

He's wearing a New England Patriots hat that says GO, PATS!

"Thanks," he says. "Nice, um, sweaters."

"Thanks."

Emma is always cold, so she wears lots of layers. Sometimes she'll wear a V-neck sweater over a crew-neck sweater and then sometimes even a cardigan sweater over that, all buttoned up. Then she makes these little slits in the cuffs so she can pull them down over her hands and she sticks her thumbs out through the holes so they're like a sweater/fingerless-glove combo. For pants, she wears leggings in different colors. All those bulky sweaters make her legs look extra skinny. She's like SpongeBob SquarePants, only she's SpongeEmma SquareSweater. But I don't tell her that. Even though she pretends not to care what people think, I know she does. Too much. My parents know this, too, but they are great at pretending it's not true.

Stu finally shows up and pushes his way into the backseat so that Emma is squished between us. As soon as we hit the road, Stu and Harper start arguing about who's going to make it to the Superbowl this year. I wish my mom would turn up the radio, but she loves to listen to carpool talk. She says it's the only way she gets any information. Emma pops her earbuds in and moves her head slightly to the music. It sounds like some kind of reggae stuff, which I can't stand. She doesn't offer to share a bud, which is fine with me. I don't know which is worse: her music, or Harper's whining about the Patriots and the New York Giants. You'd think we were talking about some upcoming war, the way he talks.

Must be nice to have your biggest worry be about whether your favorite football team makes it to the Superbowl. But I wouldn't know about that.

2

Please Don't Encourage the Cat to Lick You

"Here's what you need to know when a girl sits next to you," Ryan tells me and Sam while we eat lunch a few days later. "The first time, it was probably a mistake."

We're sitting outside on the steps, just the three of us. It's cold, but sometimes you need some fresh air. The locker-juice smell still lingers in the hall, even though it's been three days since the incident.

"What if a girl sits next to you twice?" Sam asks. He takes a small bite of a potato chip. Sam is a dainty eater. He's the only person I know who bites his chips instead of popping them in his mouth whole.

"Two times means she feels sorry for you," Ryan explains. "Probably just trying to be nice. It's a pity sit."

I pick at the Tofurky sandwich my sister made. Emma is in charge of school lunches. I'm in charge of breakfasts. I would switch if I wasn't so lazy. Emma became a vegan two years ago and refuses to make non-vegan lunches for me. She says it's against her principles to handle meat and dairy products.

"What if a girl sits with you *three* times?" I ask.

Ryan takes a drink from his water bottle. "Then you're in business."

I don't know where Ryan gets his information, but for the most part, he seems to know what he's talking about.

"So, how many times has Molly sat next to you?" I ask.

"Four," Ryan says, shaking his head.

"She must be *really* into you," Sam says. He takes another tiny bite of his chip.

Ryan sighs and glances up at the sky. "But . . . why?" he asks it.

"Are you fishing for compliments?"

He shoves me. "No. I just don't get it. I'm not her type, anyway."

"How do you know?" Sam asks seriously.

"Look at her. I mean . . . she's kind of . . . L.L.Bean catalog."

"What does that mean?"

"You know, perfectly ironed, matching clothes. Conservative. Not that there's anything wrong with that. It's just not my style."

"What catalog are you?" I ask.

"There is no catalog for me," he says proudly.

"You think you're so special," Sam says.

"No, I don't. I just . . . don't want to be that predictable, you know?"

Sam finally finishes his chip and takes a sip from his milk carton. "Not really."

"Figures a girl finally likes me and it has to be someone like Molly," he says sadly.

"I think she's nice," Sam says.

Ryan looks miserable as we follow Sam back inside after lunch. Curly is waiting in the hallway and mews at us to give her our leftovers. Cheese is her favorite. It's kind of a miracle that she's not obese.

"All I have is fake turkey," I tell her. "It would probably make you sick."

"Don't encourage her, Noah. She should only eat cat food," Sam says.

"I wasn't encouraging. I was explaining."

"Curly, you shouldn't eat food from other people's lunch," Sam tells her seriously. "You don't know who touched it or where it came from or how unhealthy it could be for you."

Curly stares up at Sam and mews sadly.

"You're bumming her out," Ryan tells him. He bends down and holds out his hand. She licks his thumb.

"That is so unsanitary," Sam says.

Curly ignores him and keeps licking until Ryan takes his hand away.

"What's wrong with it?" Ryan asks.

"Are you going to wash your hand now?"

"No."

We throw our lunch bags into our lockers and go to class. Curly follows.

"Now she's going to want to lick everyone," Sam says. "I can't believe you."

"What's wrong with licking everyone?" I ask. "Dogs do it."

"She's not a dog. She's more like . . . a wingless bat."

Curly tilts her pointy head up at us. It's hard to picture a bat wearing a hot-pink sweater-vest like the one she has on today. Of course, it should be hard to picture a naked *cat* wearing a hot-pink sweater-vest, too.

"Guess I know what's going in the Suggestion Box next," Sam says. "'No licking.'"

"You need to lighten up," Ryan tells him. "And you might want to be a little more specific if you put that note in the box."

"Why?" Sam asks.

But Ryan doesn't have the patience to explain.

Sam is an odd duck. My dad says he "lacks a filter." He says whatever pops into his head. Sometimes it's something brilliant, and other times it's just too much information. Sometimes we learn interesting stuff, like about the possibility of life on Mars, especially since Mrs. Phelps keeps telling us that global warming is happening faster than anyone predicted and in the next few decades the planet could get so hot and the storms so severe that no one will survive. But then other times we learn stuff we wish we could unlearn, like the details of Sam's poop—how often he goes, what color it is, what size it is, what *texture* it is, and what it smells like. Sam is the king of oversharing.

Ryan and I follow Sam into our language arts class and sit at the big circular table Mr. Marshall set up so the students can see one another during discussions. Today we're talking about the first half of *Lord of the Flies*. So far, this book is creepy and disturbing.

Emma says the book is going to steal away my innocence like it did hers, and that they should stop teaching it. She had to read it in middle school, too. She got in big trouble because she made a list of which of her classmates would go crazy and turn into savages if they got trapped on an island, the way most of the boys in the book do, and which wouldn't. Unfortunately, Ms. Cliff saw the list and felt the need to discuss it "anonymously" at Community Meeting. It didn't take long for everyone to figure out who she was talking about, and for a while, Emma was the most popular girl in school, not because she was the prettiest and smartest but because everyone wanted to find out if she thought they'd be a savage or a Ralph. Ralph's the main character and the only one who doesn't either die or turn into a beast follower, which is what happens to all the boys who become savages. Pretty soon, it didn't matter who she labeled what, because the whole school was fighting about it and calling one another savages and it was all Emma's fault. And just like in the book, they turned on her. Emma, who everyone loved and adored, suddenly became the outcast. I'm pretty sure she started out convinced she was a Ralph, but in the end she came to believe she was the beast after all. The entire incident changed her in a big way. It was like she'd seen how she was capable of being a terrible person without even being stranded on an island. Even though eventually people forgot about it and moved on and forgave her, Emma couldn't. She started trying to be more perfect and more adored than she was before, but to do that, she was secretly punishing herself. It's not a time we like to talk about.

Emma used to want to be a psychologist someday. I think she liked to study people to find out if they had a dark side. Sometimes when I had friends over, she'd ask them weird questions, like if they killed insects quickly or tortured them first. I'm glad no one admitted to doing anything worse than squishing a spider with a shoe (Sam) and swatting flies with one of those flyswatter guns you get from the dollar store (Ryan).

Sometimes I'd catch her watching me, like she was trying to figure out if I'd grow up to be a serial killer.

But that all stopped after the *Lord of the Flies* incident. It's really too bad, because as mean as it was to make that list, I bet she was right about a lot of people.

"Noah, what was the beast?" Mr. Marshall asks me. "Why do you think the boys all believe in its presence?"

Mr. Marshall never starts class in the usual way, like by saying hello to everyone or telling us what we're going to do that day. He just launches into a discussion as if we never stopped talking from the day before.

I think a minute before I answer. Unlike Mrs. Phelps, who gets closer and closer to your face until you answer, Mr. Marshall seems to put the whole room on pause to wait.

I think of the boys on the beach and how they all act kind of scary. Even Ralph, the one who's supposed to be the good guy.

"I think the beast is the thing inside you that makes you tempted to do bad things," I say. "It's . . . something some people have and some don't. Or maybe we all have it. When we're put into a bad situation, like being stranded on an island, the beast inside wakes up, looking for who will follow him. The boys believed in the beast because they could feel it waking up inside themselves."

"Fascinating," Mr. Marshall says. "Sadie, what do you think of that?"

Sadie looks at me and smiles shyly. "I agree with Noah."

Ryan nudges me under the table. I nudge back.

"Care to explain?" Mr. Marshall asks.

Her face turns bright red. "No," she says quietly. "Noah said it really well."

"Did you read the assignment?" he asks her.

"Yes."

"And you don't have any thoughts of your own to add?"

She shakes her head. She looks like she wants to crawl under the table.

"What about you, Lily?" Mr. Marshall asks hopefully.

Lily starts talking, but I don't really listen because Ryan slides a slip of paper over to me: *S likes u.*

I roll my eyes.

Ryan crosses out the words and draws a heart with

my and Sadie's initials in it. Sometimes I think he forgets we're not in third grade anymore.

"Ryan? You seem busy over there. Do you agree with Lily?"

"Huh? Um. Sorry?"

"What do you think of the beast?"

Ryan takes his time, then finally answers. "I think we're all beasts. This book is insane. I don't know who I'm supposed to like."

"Why do you think you're supposed to like someone?"

"Isn't that the point of books? To care about the main character so you want to keep reading?"

"Is it?"

Ryan sighs. "Who's to say?" he asks. This is the old answering-a-question-with-a-question trick. *Who's to say?* is a good way to reply to a question which you sort-of know the answer to but are not willing to expand on. Mrs. Phelps always used to answer questions with "What do *you* think?" which is honestly one of the most annoying replies ever, when you just want to know something. Then Ryan figured out to answer *that* question with "Who's to say?" which we then *all* began doing, and now she never does that anymore.

"Well, I'd like *you* to say," Mr. Marshall says.

He got him there, I guess.

"Do you want to finish the book or not?" Mr. Marshall asks.

"Only to find out if anyone is left standing."

"Then I guess the author did his job, even if you don't like any of the characters."

Mr. Marshall walks back to his desk and grabs a stack of papers. "Your next assignment is to write an expanded paragraph on the beast. Details are on the handout, but if you have any questions, ask. Due next Friday."

He hands out the papers and then starts reading from the book. It's hard to listen. We're at the part where things are going downhill fast. I'm sure if anyone is going to die, it will be Piggy, who kind of reminds me of Sam because he's so innocent and loyal. This makes me sad. Why is the trusty sidekick always the one to bite the dust?

That afternoon, Harper and Stu don't need a ride, so Emma's friend Sara gets in the car before my mom even says she can come over. It doesn't matter. It's always OK. My mom always seems so relieved when we have friends over, like she's worried we've become outcasts if we don't. The *Lord of the Flies* incident with Emma really put her on high alert.

"Do you have any dietary restrictions?" she asks Sara. My mom actually uses phrases like that.

"She's vegan, like me," Emma tells her. "But we'll cook dinner."

Great. Whenever Emma cooks dinner, we end up having to try all of her disgusting "healthy" meat alternatives.

"No seitan," I tell her. "That stuff is disgusting."

"Satan?" Sara asks.

"Not like Satan, the devil. *Seitan.* It's a meat substitute," Emma tells her. "But if you've had meat recently, you might not think it's very good. It's an acquired taste."

I will never acquire a taste for that stuff. *Satan* is definitely a more accurate way to describe it.

"Sara is new to veganism," Emma explains.

"Is your family vegan, too?" my mom asks.

"No, just me. My parents are all stressed-out about it. They think I'm going to become anemic or something."

Emma sighs dramatically, as if to say, *So typical.*

My mom clears her throat uncomfortably. "We

were worried about Emma, too. But she's very aware of her dietary needs. Right, Emma?"

"Kind of hard not to be with you and Dad obsessing about everything I eat," Emma says sarcastically.

My mom doesn't answer, just grips the steering wheel tighter. Sara shifts in her seat awkwardly, probably remembering the time a few years ago that no one talks about. Even though she and Emma weren't good friends then, everyone knows about the Thing That Happened.

When we get home, Emma takes Sara straight to her room and shuts the door. I go to my own room and figure out the minimum amount of work I have to do to get credit for it. Our dog, the Captain, carries his ratty tennis ball to me and drops it at my feet. He doesn't really like to fetch; it's just his way of letting me know he needs some love. Even though he's Emma's dog, he seems to love me best. He probably resents her for giving him a stupid name. We got him right after she'd seen this old movie called *Dead Poets Society* about an English teacher who tries to save a bunch of kids from boredom, and they all say to him "O Captain! My Captain!" when he gets fired, which is a reference to some poem, and I guess she found it really moving, so she named our dog Captain. Only somehow we all got to referring to him as *the* Captain because he's so special. And by "special" I mean no one smells like the Captain, no one snores like the Captain, and definitely no one *farts* like the Captain.

I kick the ball gently for him, and it rolls across the room. He looks up at me with his "Is that really all you've got?" look of disappointment.

"Sorry," I say. "Too much work to do." But before I can start, I get a text from Ryan asking what I'm doing. I tell him homework. A few minutes later, he calls.

"Are you done with homework yet?" he asks.

"It's been three minutes," I say.

"So, are you?"

"No?"

"I've been thinking about Molly Lo."

"Not this again."

"I decided I really don't want to go out with her."

"I already knew that," I remind him.

"I'm just not that into her," he says, ignoring me.

"I know. Too L.L.Bean."

He's quiet for a minute. "I'm just . . . not attracted. In any way."

"Are you basing this just on looks and how she dresses?"

Another pause. "No?"

I shake my head, even though he can't see me. "You really are shallow."

"I can't help it. There's no *chemistry*."

"There's one-way chemistry."

"You can't have a chemical reaction if there's nothing to charge with."

"Love isn't scientific," I tell him.

He ignores this. "Can you just tell her I'm seeing someone else?"

"No."

"Why not?"

"Because it's not true."

"You wouldn't lie for me?" He sounds genuinely shocked.

"Not really."

"Fine. I'll get Sam to do it. Jeez, you're really disappointing, Noah."

"I bet you ten bucks Sam won't do it either."

"Why not?

"Because it's *wrong*."

"Why?"

"Listen," I say. "Think. This is middle school. Saying no if a girl asks you out is not earth-shattering. Get a grip and just be honest with her."

"I don't want to hurt her feelings."

"No offense, but you're not *that* amazing. She isn't going to jump off a cliff if you say no."

He sighs heavily. "Fine, then."

"Does that mean you're not going to try to avoid her anymore? You're going to be normal from now on?"

"I guess."

"Good. I have to do my homework now."

"But you never want to do your homework."

I let the meaning of that sink in for him.

"Call me back when you're done," he says.

"All right," I say, and hang up.

But by the time I finish, Emma and Sara's vegan dinner is ready. It's also disgusting, as predicted. Even Emma slips half her food to the Captain, who waits patiently under the table. Only, after dinner when we're cleaning up and my mom finds the uneaten seitan on the floor, I get blamed. The Captain looks at me guiltily, but I really can't fault him for coughing it out. Emma doesn't confess her part in all this, and since

I'm not a rat, I end up having to do extra cleanup as punishment.

"Hey, thanks for not telling on me," she says later, coming into my room to say good night. She's always done this since we were little. We used to read together before bed, but now I'm too old for that.

"I thought you loved seitan," I tell her. "Why didn't you eat it?"

She gives me a strange look and shrugs. "I wasn't hungry. Never mind. I just wanted to say thanks."

"Emma," I say. "You're OK, right? You really just weren't hungry?"

She makes a disgusted face. "Not you, too, Noah! Jeez. I wish everyone would get off my case."

"What do you mean?"

"Never mind!" She stomps off down the hall.

"Emma?" I hear my mom call from her bedroom. "Is everything OK?"

"Leave me alone!" she yells.

The Captain, who has been sleeping on the floor next to my bed, gives me a worried look.

"She's just in a mood," I say, trying to reassure him.

But when I try to fall asleep, I think about the Thing

We Don't Talk About and wonder if it could be happening again. Emma sees a therapist once a week, and I try to convince myself that if something was wrong, her therapist would know and make everything better. But I'm not really sure it's that simple. I mean, I know it's not.

When I finally do fall asleep, I get woken up about every hour by a horrible smell that only the Captain is capable of producing. I guess he managed to swallow some of the seitan after all and it did *not* agree with him. If Satan has a smell, I think this is it.

3

Please Fix the Lighting in the Boys' Bathroom So We Can See Our Reflections Better

"Did yesterday never happen?" I ask Ryan as we hide out in the bathroom again. "I thought we decided you were gonna be a man about this."

"You can leave if you want, but I'm not going out there." He walks over to the mirror and squints. "Why is it so dark in here, anyway?"

"So you won't obsess over your face for five hours?"

"Ha. We need to do something about this. Write a suggestion."

"I don't think so."

"Listen. Tell me when lunch is over and the coast is clear so I can come out."

"That doesn't even make sense. You're in the same class after lunch."

"Molly's not going to ask me to go out with her in class."

"She could pass you a note."

"Ugh! Do you think she would do that? Great. Now what am I going to do?"

"Say no."

"But I'll feel bad!"

"Then say yes!"

"But I don't like her!"

I slap my forehead. "I'm going out there before this smell starts to rub off on me. If she asks me where you are, I'm telling her you're alone in here and she should come find you."

"You wouldn't."

I stare.

"You would?"

"Just come on," I say. "This place is foul."

"It wasn't me!"

"I don't care who it was. I'm going to puke if we don't get out of here." I grab his arm and drag him out. The hall is empty because everyone's still at lunch.

"Let's eat outside," Ryan says.

"It's raining," I remind him.

"I know. That means she won't be out there."

I roll my eyes but follow him anyway. It's only drizzling, so we sit on the steps and eat our sandwiches. I can tell my butt is going to have a wet spot, but anything is better than that bathroom.

After a few minutes, Sam joins us.

"I wondered where you two went," he says. "Why are you sitting in the rain?"

"Molly," I tell him.

Sam shakes his head. "She's going to track you down eventually, you know. You need to get it over with. Rip off the Band-Aid."

Ryan shrugs. "Ripping off the Band-Aid hurts."

"Yup, but the faster you do it, the faster it's over," Sam says.

"I never rip off my Band-Aids. I wait until they get wet and lose their stick and fall off."

"That explains a lot about you," I say.

"Maybe I could do something really awful in front of her so she doesn't like me."

"Such as?"

"I don't know. I could fart?"

"Then you'd make *everyone* not like you," I say.

"Good point," Ryan says. "Everyone hates the Fart Squad."

"This is no way to live," Sam says, opening his lunch bag.

As soon as he pulls out his sandwich, a horrible smell wafts over us. Ryan gags. I cough.

"What. Is. THAT?" Ryan asks, sliding away from him.

"Liverwurst and onions. And some mustard," Sam says. "What's wrong?"

"Can't you smell it?" I say, sliding the other way.

"Yes. It smells *great*!" Sam says, sniffing.

"What is liverwurst, anyway?" Ryan asks.

"It's a kind of sausage. You know. Made from liver."

"I think I just threw up in my mouth," I say. "Who eats liver voluntarily?"

"Most people?" Sam takes a massive bite.

"You insist on nibbling your potato chips but you'll stuff your face with liver product?"

"It's delicious! You should try it!"

"I don't think I could get my face close enough to that smell," Ryan says.

"You guys are missing out," Sam says with his mouth full.

"That must give you some seriously bad breath," I tell him.

"That's what mints are for. My mom puts them in my lunch whenever she makes me something that will give me bad breath."

"I don't think mints can hide that stench," Ryan says. "No offense."

"Quick," I say to Ryan. "Take a bite of Sam's sandwich and then go breathe on Molly. All your problems will be solved."

"I'm trying to be a vegan!" Ryan yells.

"Since when?"

"Emma talked me into it last time I was at your house, remember?"

I roll my eyes. "You'd do anything for her."

He doesn't deny it.

Sam holds out the sandwich for him. "I'm sure Emma would understand this one time."

Ryan takes the sandwich from Sam and lifts up

the bread to inspect the meat. "What type of animal's liver is it?"

"I think it has ham and veal livers," Sam says. He pushes his glasses up his nose the way he always does when he's providing information about something.

"Veal?" Ryan asks. "You mean, baby cow?"

"It's a delicacy," Sam explains.

"What would Emma say to *that*?" I ask, shaking my head.

"You're right," Ryan says. "I can't do it."

"I won't tell," Sam says.

"Even so . . . it's a baby cow!" Ryan says.

"Just the liver," Sam clarifies.

Ryan looks at me for advice, but I don't have any.

He plugs his nose with his free hand. "Noah, do you have anything left in your water bottle?"

I shake it. "A little."

"Be ready. I'm gonna need it."

I hug it to my chest. "No way are you putting your baby-cow-liver mouth on my water bottle!"

"You two are totally overreacting. It's delicious!" Sam says.

"One . . . two . . ." Ryan is just about to take a bite

when the door swings open and Molly steps out with Lily and Belle.

"Hey, guys," Molly says.

Ryan quickly hands the sandwich back to Sam.

"We're putting together a playlist for the dance and wanted to get your requests," Belle says. "Everyone is allowed to give three suggestions."

"What dance?" Sam asks.

"It's next Friday, remember?"

"Oh. I forgot." Sam takes another bite of his sandwich.

"What's that smell?" Belle asks.

Sam and I look at Ryan. He *could* say it's him and maybe gross Molly out. But instead he points to the sandwich like a traitor.

"What?" Sam says. "I think it smells good."

"What kind of sandwich is that?" Lily asks, wrinkling her nose.

Sam sighs. "Liverwurst and onions. With mustard."

"Gross," Belle says. "No offense."

It seems like we all say "No offense" a lot around Sam.

"My grandfather used to make those!" Molly leans forward and sniffs. "Can I have a bite?"

Sam looks shocked. "Really? Yeah!" He hands it over and she takes a huge bite, nodding as she chews.

"Oh, yeah," she says through a mouthful. "Mmmm." She smiles at Sam as if this is the first time she's noticed him. "He made these for me whenever I visited him."

Molly hands what's left of the sandwich back to Sam, who smiles at her dreamily.

Ryan watches them in disbelief as they fall in love over a liverwurst sandwich.

"Can we get back to the music requests?" Lily asks, ignoring them. She's holding a notebook and pencil.

"What do you have so far?" I ask.

She shrugs. "The usual. Oh, and 'Stairway to Heaven.' The teachers make us play that last at every dance."

"That song goes on forever!" Ryan says.

"It's a tradition," Lily says. "Do you have any requests or not? It's cold out here. And smelly. No offense."

"No country," Ryan says.

"Or dubstep," I add.

"But a bunch of people have requested that already."

"If a bunch of people request *not* to have it, will that cancel it out?"

"I don't know," Lily says.

"I think it should," Belle says. I think she smiles at me, but I'm not sure. Could Belle like me? She turns away before I can decide if it was a pity smile.

"Fine. I'll keep track," Lily says.

"Well, I'm with Noah, so that's two against," Ryan says.

Sam stands up. "Me too."

Lily makes some marks in her notebook. "Got it."

Sam reaches in his lunch bag and pulls out a tin of mints. He takes one and offers the tin to Molly, who blushes.

We all start to go inside, but Ryan stays back and grabs my arm before we go in.

"Did you see that?" he asks excitedly. "I think I'm free!"

"Yes," I say. "Congratulations. Saved by liverwurst."

"And onions," Ryan adds. "Can you believe it?"

"Love at first bite," I say. We both crack up.

Ryan puts his arm over my shoulder. "C'mon," he says happily. "Art's next. I know that's your favorite."

"You do?"

"Sure. You're, like, the best artist in the school."

"Really?" I never knew he even noticed my stuff.

"Just don't let it go to your head. No one likes a show-off." He lets go of my shoulder and hurries ahead.

This month we've been using clay in art. At first I didn't like it. It smells funny and is kind of hard to work with. But then Ms. Cliff showed me this cool technique for wetting the clay just the right amount and using the ribbon tool to shave off extra clay to shape it smooth.

One time when we were studying Michelangelo, we learned that when he worked with stone, he chipped it away to set the image free. It sort of feels like that when I'm using the ribbon. When I start with a chunk of clay, I'm not sure what I'm going to make. But as I play with it and begin to peel away the outside, an image forms. I've never told anyone this, but Ms. Cliff told me she thinks I have a real gift for sculpting. No one ever tells me I have a gift for anything. Most adults don't even notice me. Emma's the one with all the gifts. Only . . . when I'm working with the clay, I finally feel like there's something I can do that she can't. It's like this secret no one else knows, except for Ms. Cliff. And now I guess maybe Ryan. I don't know why, but it makes me feel good. When I'm working with clay and a shape starts to emerge, I feel like someone else. Not Emma's little brother, or Ryan and Sam's best friend. I'm just Noah. Maybe I don't tell anyone about it because I'm not sure they'd understand what I mean. Or maybe I don't tell them because I don't want them to understand. I know that sounds sort of dumb, but it's true. When I'm in the art room, smelling the clay, shaping something out of nothing, nothing else matters. I can forget everything else and just focus on creating something new.

Ryan glances over at me as I start to use the ribbon. He holds up his sculpture, which looks like a misshapen bowl, and rolls his eyes. I smile and get back to my own work, shutting everything else out. For the rest of class, I am lost in the clay in my hands, far away from school and worrying about who has crushes on who and homework and the science test coming up, but most of all, I am far away from home and from worrying about the Thing That Happened and whether it could happen again.

4

The Pole in the Community Room Is Not for Pole Dancing

The day of the dance, everyone at school acts even more hyper than usual. During lunch, Zach Bray goes over to one of the structural poles in the Community Room and starts pole dancing like he's at a strip club or something.

Sasha, Belle, and Molly squeal and tell him he's gross.

Ryan claps and woots for more, then holds out a dollar for him.

"You really shouldn't encourage him," Sam says, all serious.

Zach ignores him and takes the dollar. He shoves it down his shirt as if he has a bra on under it.

"You two are disgusting," Belle says to them.

Lily comes up next to her. "That is so degrading to women," she says, crossing her arms at her chest.

"You're just jealous because you don't have my moves," Zach tells her.

"Right," Lily says.

"Is that a challenge?" Zach steps away from the pole and gestures for her to take a turn.

"In your dreams," Lily says.

"How'd you know?" Zach looks her up and down.

"Belle's right. You are disgusting."

Zach clutches his heart dramatically and falls on the floor. "You hurt me, Lily! You hurt me so bad!"

Lily rolls her eyes and walks away.

Zach reaches his hand out to Ryan, who pulls him up.

"I'm totally asking Lily to the dance now," Zach says.

"Good idea." Ryan smacks him on the back.

"Seriously?" I ask.

"She is *so* into me."

"OK," I say doubtfully.

"C'mon, you saw how she was looking at me."

"She kind of looked like she wanted to throw up," Sam says.

Zach ignores him and goes back to the pole, dancing again to some song in his head that clearly makes him feel like a dance god.

Sam and Ryan come to my house after school so we can all go to the dance together. Even though Sam is "taking" Molly to the dance, it doesn't mean they actually arrive together. It just means that they plan to be at the dance as a couple.

Ryan keeps saying how relieved he is, but the more thrilled Sam acts, the less convincing Ryan seems, and I'm starting to wonder if he's having second thoughts about Molly after all.

"I think you need new pants," Sam tells Ryan, who is standing in front of the mirror that hangs on the back of my bedroom door.

The Captain keeps circling his legs, trying to herd him to the bed to sit down.

"Why do I need new pants?" Ryan asks, twisting so he can see his butt.

"They're a little tight," Sam says.

"They're supposed to look like this. It's the style."

"Are you turning into an emu?" Sam asks.

"A what?"

"Emu. You know. A guy who wears eyeliner and tight pants and acts depressed." Sam pushes his glasses up his nose.

"I think you mean *emo*," I say.

Ryan cracks up.

"Yes," Sam says, not seeing what's so funny.

"Do I look emo? Am I wearing guyliner?"

Sam frowns. "I don't know. It's kind of dark in here."

"You need overhead lights," Ryan tells me. "Why don't you have any lights in here?"

I shrug. "I don't need to stare at myself with the same intensity as you."

"Ha."

"I don't really get what emo is," I say. "You're supposed to be serious all the time and not think anything is funny, right? Or . . . you're only supposed to be friends with other guys who wear tight pants and eyeliner?"

"This is the problem with living in a small town," Ryan says. "We don't know anything."

Sam holds out his phone with a Wikipedia entry for emo. "I guess you're not really one. You're not *morose* enough."

"You can call me emu, though," Ryan says. "That's a great nickname."

The Captain licks his hand. Ryan wipes the spit on his jeans, finishes adjusting his T-shirt over his hips just so, and flops down on my bed next to Sam.

I go over to the mirror and take in my own jeans-and-T-shirt ensemble. I am on the short side and still can't fit into guy sizes. It's kind of mortifying because they don't have any cool styles of jeans for "boys." My choices are "husky" or "slim." It's ridiculous.

"Does Molly send you texts?" Ryan asks, bouncing on the bed.

Sam holds his phone to his chest.

"Let me see-ee," Ryan sings.

"No, it's private."

"We're best friends! C'mon!" He grabs for the phone. The Captain barks.

"I said it's private!" Sam shoves the phone under his shirt.

"You think I won't reach under there?" Ryan asks, reaching.

Sam hugs himself tighter. "Respect my personal space, please!"

Sometimes Sam talks like he's still in kindergarten.

"I'm just messing with you. Don't worry." Ryan backs off. "Just summarize."

"She only says stuff like 'See you tomorrow' or whatever. It's nothing lovey-dovey."

"Well, you *have* been dating less than a week," I say. "Give her time."

"Do you know how to slow-dance, by the way?" Ryan asks. "Because if you're going to the dance as a couple, you know that means you have to dance to every song together, right?"

Sam looks up at the ceiling. "I know. It's kind of why my hands are sweating right now."

"Gross! Don't touch my comforter," I say.

He wipes his palms on his pants. "I'm the worst dancer in the world. Will you teach me?"

"To slow-dance?" Ryan asks. "How are we supposed to teach you that?"

"You could"—Sam looks around as if there could possibly be anyone else in the room—"*show* me. You know." He blushes.

"I think I do, but no." Ryan gets up and crosses the room to the chair at my desk. The Captain waddles after him.

"But you're the only one who knows how!"

"Hey!" I say. "Maybe I know how."

"Will you teach me, then?"

"No. Sorry. Ryan should do it. He's the emu."

"What's that supposed to mean?" Ryan asks.

"Actually, I have no idea," I tell him.

"C'mon, you guys, please? I won't tell anyone, I promise."

"No way," I say. "I can just imagine someone posting a video of us dancing together online."

"Who would do that?" Sam asks.

I look over at Ryan.

"No trust," he says. "You're supposed to be my best friends."

Sam inches his butt to the edge of the bed and looks up at Ryan in his innocent way. "Best friends help each other."

"Just do it," I tell Ryan. "*I* won't tell anyone."

"Fine." Ryan walks over to Sam and holds out his arms.

"You're a good friend," I tell him.

I don't have any slow songs on my playlist, so they make me download "Stairway to Heaven."

"I'll be the girl," Ryan says as the music starts. He puts his hands on Sam's shoulders.

"What do I do?" Sam asks.

"Put your hands on my waist. But don't get too close. You have to let the girl be the one to move in."

"That's sexist."

"Why?" I ask.

"You are assigning male and female roles," Sam explains.

"Just trust me," Ryan says. "You may think it's sexist, but if you try to get too close, she might slap you."

They start to pivot awkwardly. I admit, I'm tempted to take a picture.

"You have to sway, not just pick up your feet," Ryan says. "Like this." He moves his hips a little.

Sam looks down between Ryan's arms to watch his hips. "I can't do that!"

"Why not? It's easy! Feel my hips. See how I move them to the beat?"

Sam wiggles his butt, but he looks more like he's belly dancing than moving to a slow song.

Ryan starts to laugh.

"What's so funny?" Sam asks. He wiggles again, and Ryan lets go and falls on the floor in hysterics. The Captain bounds over to him and starts doing an embarrassing thing dogs do to people when they are lying on the floor sometimes.

"Ack! Get off me!" Ryan yells, rolling over.

The Captain barks excitedly.

Sam watches himself wiggle his hips in the mirror. "What am I doing wrong?" he asks, all serious.

I crack up, too.

"It's not funny!" he says. "This is serious! My first chance at a girlfriend, and I'm gonna screw it up!"

"It's not that dire," I say when I finally stop laughing.

"Easy for you to say."

"Why?"

"You're not . . . me."

I don't ask what that means, because I'm pretty sure I know. Sam is a little chunky. Definitely a former "husky" wearer. He's also a little awkward and a little smelly. Sad as it is, sometimes those things get in the way of seeing how great a person really is.

My bedroom door opens, and Emma steps in without knocking. The Captain leaves Ryan and trots over to her. She pats his head. "Why are you guys listening to 'Stairway to Heaven'?" she asks.

"Hey, Emma," Ryan says, trying to act all cool.

"Yeah, hey," Sam says. "So, um. I need to learn how to slow-dance." He looks down at the rug and rubs his foot back and forth nervously. He has a hole in his sock and his big toe sticks out a little. He doesn't seem to notice.

Emma studies him for a minute. "Why do you want to learn?"

Sam digs his toe deeper into the carpet. "Well . . ."

"He has a date," I say.

"That's awesome!" She claps her hands. "Do you want me to help? But you have to pick a different song. I hate this one."

Sam glows. "Yes, please!"

"Let me go get some music!" She runs to her room.

Sam turns to both of us with his mouth wide open in a cross between a smile and a look of absolute shock.

Kind of like what I imagine *I* would look like if I won the lottery.

"Your sister is the best!" Sam says.

I roll my eyes.

Ryan flops on the bed. "Sam gets all the ladies."

"You both need to stop drooling over my sister," I say. "And never refer to her as a lady. God."

"Everyone drools over her," Ryan says. "It can't be helped."

"You could've gone out with Molly, but you blew it," Sam tells him.

Ryan falls back on the bed as if he's been shot.

"You two are pathetic." I flop onto the oversize beanbag chair Emma gave me for Christmas last year and listen to the Styrofoam beads inside settle under me.

"I'm just a lonely emu," Ryan says.

Emma comes back and plugs her music into my stand.

"What is it?" Sam asks.

"Lynyrd Skynyrd," Emma says.

"Who?"

"You know. 'Free Bird'? They *always* play this song at dances."

"I don't think anyone gave that title to Lily."

Emma shrugs. "The Tank always makes the DJs play this song. Trust me." She steps closer to Sam. "OK, Sammy. Come over here and let me show you how it's done."

Sam hates that nickname with a passion. Unless, of course, it's coming out of Emma's mouth while she holds her arms open to him like she's going to give him a big hug.

"Put your hands on my hips," Emma tells Sam, stepping closer and putting her hands on his shoulders.

Sam looks like he's about to faint.

"You can't be shy," Emma says, reaching for his hands.

She's wearing her usual SpongeBob outfit of layers of sweaters and a pair of leggings.

"Noah, hit play," Emma tells me. She leans closer to Sam. "Just listen to the words and move to the story. Don't think about the beat." They start to sway really slowly.

As I listen to the words, I get this sad feeling. The song is about having to leave someone you love because you know you can't change. The singer tells the story in this really hopeless, final way. It seems like the *last* song you'd want to dance to with a girl you're just starting to date.

Emma closes her eyes and rests her head on Sam's shoulder. Ryan shakes his head, like he cannot believe Sam's luck. But Sam doesn't actually look like he's enjoying it all that much. He has this weird expression on his face, as if he's trying not to step on glass.

"C'mon, Sam. *Hold me*," Emma says. She moves closer to him and makes him put his arms around her.

If it's possible to die of discomfort, Sam is in imminent danger.

"Just sway a bit more, like this," Emma tells him, swaying.

Sam holds his arms stiffly and rocks back and forth like a zombie, without bending his legs.

Then the music speeds up and Sam looks even more horrified than he did before. "What do we do now?" he asks in a panic. "I can't fast-dance!"

Emma laughs. "The trick is to pretend that the music is still slow. Everyone *else* might start dancing faster, but *you* just keep your date in your arms like this and move real slow, like you're in your own world."

"But—isn't that kind of weird?" Sam asks.

Emma laughs again. "No. I promise. Your date will love it. She'll think you are in some kind of love zone together."

"Love zone?"

She steps away from him before the song is totally over and sings about the bird you can't change as she walks out the door. As if she is the bird, and she cannot change.

Sam drops on the bed next to Ryan. "Wow."

"Shut up," Ryan says. "I don't even want to hear about it."

I put my own music back on and try to ignore their lovestruck faces, but it gets to be a bit much, so I leave them to go get something for us to eat.

In the kitchen, my dad is busy putting something together for dinner. I look in the cupboard where we keep bags of chips and stuff, but all I can find is a bag of Emma's gross organic corn chips. Emma insists we buy organic everything. Her idea of a fun snack treat is dried-up vegetables made to look like french fries that taste like lightly salted air.

"Don't we have anything else?" I ask my dad. "I'm starving."

"You're hungry, not starving," my dad corrects. "Take the corn chips. They're not that bad."

I grab the bag and groan when I see they're unsalted on top of everything else.

"Don't start, Noah," my dad warns. Rule of the house: Never complain about food. Don't even talk about food. Just eat it.

"Do we at least have some salsa?"

"We might, but if we do, you're not taking it to your room. It's bad enough you eat chips up there."

I take the bag and go back upstairs. When I reach my room, I can hear Ryan and Sam talking inside.

"I'm serious," Sam says. "It was kind of creepy."

"You get to put your hands on Emma's hips and all you can say is it was creepy?" Ryan asks. "She's just a little thin, that's all."

"What if she's . . . you know. Sick again."

"She seems fine to me."

I make a point of crinkling the bag so they hear me before I join them.

They both jump and look guilty, but I pretend not to notice and hold out the bag. The Captain whines at me for some.

"They don't even have salt," I tell him. "Don't waste your time."

Sam takes a nibble. "Kind of bland."

"Don't start," I warn him. Sam and Ryan know the rules, too. But it's something they don't talk about, either. At least not to my face.

We pass the bag around and eat the whole thing, even though it tastes like wood shavings.

"I really hope this dance isn't lame," Ryan says, brushing crumbs off his jeans onto the floor. The Captain immediately starts licking them up.

"I heard there's good food," Sam says.

"I just hope there's no dubstep. I really hate that crap," Ryan says.

"Yeah, me too," Sam agrees. "Who are you guys going to ask to dance?"

Ryan smiles. "Like I'd tell."

"Like you would dare to ask anyone," I say.

"True enough."

Sam pats Ryan's shoulder reassuringly, as if he's suddenly the experienced one. "Don't worry: I'm sure someone will ask you guys to dance."

"Don't hold your breath." I pick up the empty

bag of chips and throw it into the trash basket under my desk.

Ryan turns up the music and starts dancing around the room like a maniac, making the Captain bark and Sam howl with laughter. I sit at my desk and watch, trying to focus on my friends instead of worrying about what I heard them say about Emma.

But it doesn't really work. All I can think about is the "Free Bird" song and how Emma sang the words like they were written just for her. And what it means if she's a bird we can't change, no matter how hard we try.

5

Please Ban Country Music from All Future Dances

"You boys behave yourselves," my dad tells us when he drops us off at the school. "And don't forget your cans!"

Ryan, Sam, and I grab the shopping bag full of canned vegetables my dad gathered for us. Instead of paying to get into the dance, we have to donate three cans each for the local food bank. Ryan hauls his bag over his shoulder.

"Let's get this over with," he says, like we're on some kind of mission.

We start to cross the parking lot before we realize

that Sam is still standing next to the car. We stop and turn back.

"What?" Ryan asks.

"I'm not sure I can do this."

"Oh, gimme a break. This isn't your high-school prom. Get ahold of yourself." Ryan grabs Sam's arm and drags him forward.

Molly is waiting for Sam at the steps outside. She smiles shyly.

"Hi, Sam," she says. She doesn't say hi to me or Ryan.

"Huh-hi," Sam says. "You look . . . pretty."

She blushes. She's wearing more makeup than usual, and her hair is curled in these long coil things instead of pulled back like usual. Ryan stares at her with his mouth open as if he's never seen her before. I don't usually like it when girls curl their hair like that, but I have to admit she does look nice. She's also wearing a sparkly dress that I'm pretty sure you can't get from an L.L.Bean catalog. Still, I think I prefer the original Molly.

Lily, who was waiting with Molly, ignores us, craning her neck toward the parking lot to see if anyone better has arrived. Either that or she's waiting for her own date. If she said yes to Zach, I'll puke.

Ryan and I leave them and go inside.

The dance is in the Community Room. The couches have been moved along one wall, and there's a sad excuse for a disco ball hanging from the middle of the ceiling. It looks like someone glued silver sequins to a big Styrofoam ball. On closer inspection, I see I'm right.

A few eighth-graders sit behind a table in the corner with a laptop and some speakers. They're the DJs, I guess. There's another table loaded with bowls of chips and bottles of soda.

"Well, this looks like fun," Ryan says sarcastically. "Tell me why we're here again?"

I glance around the room and spot Zach, who is already dancing with the pole.

"That?" I ask.

"Let's just get some food," Ryan says, disappointed.

As I pour myself some Mountain Dew, I notice Curly poking her head out from under one of the couches. She must wonder what we're all doing back here, invading her usual quiet time. She doesn't seem too happy about it.

Ryan and I take our drinks and napkins piled with

chips to an empty couch. As more people arrive, they stand around in clusters to talk. No one dances. Every so often a good part in the song comes on and people do a mini-move, halfheartedly, and then go back to talking.

"What do you think of Sadie Darrow?" Ryan asks under his breath.

We both look over at Sadie, standing with Lily, Belle, Molly, Sam (who looks like he is having the time of his life all of a sudden), and Tate Channing, a long-haired eighth-grader.

"She's cute," I say. "But . . . is it just me, or does she kind of look like a guy?"

"Because she has short hair? It's called a pixie cut," Ryan explains. "They're popular in the real world."

Tate grabs Sadie and hugs her. Lily just stands there, still craning her neck around looking for cool people while Sam and Molly smile goofily at each other and hold hands.

"I think Sadie looks like a boy because of Tate," I say as I watch them hugging.

Ryan studies them. "Yeah, you're right. When you can't see their faces, you'd guess Sadie was the boy and Tate the girl. Man. We are such stereotypers."

Usually Tate wears his hair down his back in a braid, but tonight he's wearing it loose and it's all wavy and a little too perfect. I wonder if he curled it with the same kind of special curling iron Molly used.

Some terrible country song comes on, and Tate drags Sadie onto the dance floor. Every so often, Tate flicks his head so his hair swishes over his shoulder and bounces. He looks like he's auditioning for a shampoo commercial.

"It's nothing personal," Ryan says. "I have nothing against guys who grow their hair out. Whatever. But I really can't stand *that* guy's hair."

"That's because he's dancing with Sadie," I say.

"He's such a jerk." Ryan imitates the hair flick. "Plus he has terrible taste in music. Please."

"Don't be mean," I say, silently thinking the same thing.

As predicted, "Free Bird" eventually comes on, and Sam and Molly walk slowly to the dance floor. They've already slow-danced a few times to other songs, looking as awkward as we thought they would. But this time, Sam walks out on the floor holding Molly's hand with a new air of confidence. Ryan notices, too, and we both sit up a little, curious to see what will happen.

Sam glances over at us and nods, as if to say, "Watch this, emos."

Sam puts his hands on Molly's hips. Unlike earlier in the night, when she kept a far distance with her hands on his shoulders, keeping her body an arm's length apart, now she moves in closer and hugs him, so their bodies are pressed against each other. She rests her head on his shoulder.

Next to them, Sadie and Tate are pressed together so tightly, they look like one person. Tate's hair hangs over Sadie's shoulder, and we get a glimpse of what Sadie would look like if she had long hair. It's kind of disturbing, though, knowing it isn't hers.

Zach and Lily are dancing, too, but you can tell Lily has made it clear they will *not* be close-dancing. Zach looks bored, but at least he's better off than me and Ryan.

Belle and Miranda-with-the-Always-Stuffed-Up-Nose are dancing really close, too. I didn't know either of them liked girls, but I guess so. I wonder how Belle can stand the constant sniffling, but it's definitely not seeming to bother her now.

At the part in the song where the fast music kicks in, Sam follows Emma's advice and keeps moving the same slow speed as if he's in a love-dance trance. Molly lifts her head once to look at him, smiles, and puts her head back on his shoulder. Everyone else tries to move faster, not knowing how to handle the unexpected change in tempo, but Sam looks as cool as a cucumber.

Emma is always right.

I listen to the words again and think about how Emma sang them as she waltzed out of my room, as if they were all about her. And I get that sinking, worried feeling I always get when I think about Emma, and what can and can't change.

Ryan crosses his arms at his chest and scowls at Sam and Molly.

"Jealous," I say.

"Of what?"

But before I can answer, someone screams.

Lily jumps onto one of the couches and points to a corner of the room.

Everyone looks, and then there are more screams.

Ryan and I get up and try to see what's going on. Someone turns off the music just as Lynyrd Skynyrd starts howling about being the bird you can't change.

"Killer!" Zach says, and jumps up and down.

I crane my neck over Ryan's shoulder and finally

see what everyone else does: Curly, standing proudly, with a mouse wriggling in her mouth.

She shakes her head violently and the mouse dangles and swirls, trying to break free. It makes a sad and desperate squeak.

The Tank runs over and tries to catch Curly, but she darts out of the way, the mouse still in her mouth. People scream one by one as she gets close to them, and soon almost everyone is standing on couches, clutching one another.

"Don't panic!" the Tank yells, panicking. "Everyone just stay calm!"

Curly trots onto the dance floor and looks at all of us. She holds her head up high and flicks her tail proudly.

A few people say "Ew." And "Gross." And "Save the mouse, Mr. Sticht!"

Curly looks confused, as if she doesn't understand why no one is saying, "Good girl!"

She drops the mouse at her feet and licks her paw. She's wearing a pink sequined camouflage vest that sparkles in the disco-ball light.

At first, it seems like the mouse is dead. But then it moves a tiny bit. Just a little twitch.

Curly stops licking and watches.

The mouse brings one paw forward and tries to drag itself forward very slowly, as if it doesn't think Curly will notice.

But then it squeaks pitifully, as if to say, "Help."

"Do something!" Lily yells. "It's suffering!"

The Tank creeps toward Curly as if he's on one of his secret missions in Iraq. Everyone gets very quiet. Curly looks up at him suspiciously, but then focuses on the mouse again. She reaches forward and pokes it with her paw.

The mouse drags itself forward another centimeter. It's so sad, watching the mouse try to get away, even though it must know it doesn't stand a chance.

I step off the couch and move slowly toward the mouse and Curly from the opposite direction of the Tank. Ryan moves in, too, from the other side. Once we're surrounding her, we carefully move closer. The mouse squeaks another SOS.

Curly's eyes dart back and forth from each of us, daring us to come closer. I take another step and she picks up the mouse in her mouth again.

There are several gasps and more *ew*s.

"Squeak."

Slowly, I take another step forward. "Good girl," I say quietly.

Curly looks up at me and makes a funny noise. Like a half purr, half mew. The mouse hangs limply.

"Good Curly," I say again, stepping closer.

Suddenly, the Tank swoops in from behind her as she's concentrating on me and wraps his enormous hands around her. He shakes her, and the mouse falls to the floor. Curly wriggles to get free.

"Get the mouse!" the Tank yells at me and Ryan.

I run to the food table and grab a plastic cup and a paper plate, the tools Emma uses to save ants, spiders, and anything else that gets inside the house that she wants to trap and let go outside. I dash back to the mouse and put the cup over it, safely protecting it from Curly.

The Tank puts her back down, and she prances over to me and meows at the cup.

I can feel everyone watching. I carefully slide the plate under the cup, having to shove it a few times when the edge touches the mouse. The mouse doesn't move.

My stomach churns, and I feel like I'm going to throw up.

When I'm sure the body is on the plate, I scoop it up and hold it out to the Tank.

"C'mon," he says quietly. "Let's take it to my room and see what we can do."

Ryan, Curly, and I are the only ones who follow him.

A few people clap as we leave, but it's not to make us feel like heroes or anything, and I'm glad.

The music comes back on as we start down the hall. Curly makes these funny chirping noises as she trots behind us, like she thinks we're taking the mouse to her food bowl.

"Never knew you were a killer," Ryan tells her.

I stop and look down at the murderer and see that her sparkly pink camo vest has blood on it.

She chirps again and runs after the Tank, holding her head up high.

6

Sequined Camouflage Is Not Appropriate at School

"Sorry, Killer, you're not invited," the Tank says, shutting the door to his classroom before Curly can saunter in.

She mews from the other side.

"Is it dead yet?" Ryan asks, pointing to the cup on the paper plate.

"Not sure," the Tank says.

Even though he teaches social studies, the Tank loves nature. He has all kinds of cages and things in his classroom, including a fish tank. Sometimes he finds dead animals on the road and brings them to school fresh for Mrs. Phelps, who then dissects them in front of us. It's always equally gross and fascinating.

"OK, little guy. Let's have a look." The Tank lifts the cup and inspects the mouse, which is very still on the paper plate.

"Hm," he says.

"What?" I ask.

"He's dead," Ryan explains.

"Are you sure?"

We peer over the tiny body, waiting for it to move. He has these cute little black beads for eyes, and tiny paws that look almost like hands. He seems to be smiling, except that there is a little bit of blood coming out of his mouth. I don't know why I think he's a boy, but I do. We wait and wait for him to twitch, but he doesn't.

"Sorry, guys. We did our best," the Tank says.

"I don't think I'll ever be able to look at Curly the same way again," Ryan says.

The Tank scratches his chin. "It's her nature. She's a cat. She was just doing her job." He looks around the room as if to make sure no one will overhear what he's about to tell us. "Can I trust you guys not to share something?"

We nod.

"The thing is," he says quietly, "Curly is a mass murderer. I find a mouse in here almost every morning. She leaves them by my desk. If it weren't for Curly, we'd probably have a real infestation on our hands. But she keeps the situation under control."

"Wow," Ryan says, impressed.

"That's just between us, remember. I'm not sure how the other students would feel if they knew."

"Right," Ryan says. "We won't tell."

"Noah?" the Tank says. "What's wrong? You've been awfully quiet."

I swallow, trying to get rid of the ache in my throat. It's the kind you get when you're trying not to cry. I don't know why I have it now. It's only a mouse. But for some reason, I feel sorry for him. I can't get the image of him trying to crawl away to safety out of my head. I look down at his cute little face again. Stupid Curly. "Nothing," I finally answer.

The Tank pats my shoulder. "Why don't you two go back to the dance? I'll take care of this little guy."

"What are you going to do with him?" Ryan asks.

"Bag him and bring him home to Stan."

"Stan?"

"My snake. He loves the things, but they have to be somewhat fresh. Curly's his main supplier."

"Wow," Ryan says.

The Tank walks over to his desk and opens a drawer. He pulls out a box of plastic sandwich bags and brings one over to the mouse. He folds the paper plate just so, slides the mouse into the bag, and zips it sealed.

"I'll just run this out to my car," he says. "See you boys back there in a jiffy."

As soon as he opens the classroom door, Curly runs over to him and looks up expectantly.

"Good girl," he says, and bends down to scratch her head.

"Wow," Ryan says again when the Tank is gone.

Curly comes over to me and rubs against my leg. I bend down and take off her vest, and then put it in the trash can next to the Tank's desk. "We shouldn't let her wear camo," I say. "It will only encourage her to hunt."

"Why don't you want her to kill mice?" Ryan asks. "She's doing this old school a service."

"I don't know."

I know it's natural for Curly to do, but I just don't like it. I don't like how the whole thing made me feel.

Helpless.

Again.

And that's all I want to say about that.

We go back to the dance and flop on the couch to people-watch.

Sam and Molly are holding hands. Zach is dancing with the pole again, but this time Lily is laughing at him in a flirty way. Pathetic.

When the next slow song comes on, Ryan leans back on the couch and stares at the ceiling like he can't bear to watch all the couples close-dancing again. I do the same. Wads of gum are stuck up there in a patternless cluster. I never noticed them before. I wonder how they got there and how long they've been hanging above us, waiting to lose their stick and land on our heads. I wonder who put them there and why they bothered.

While I'm having these deep thoughts, someone taps my knee. Sadie is standing right in front of me, smiling.

"Wanna dance?" she asks.

"Me?"

She nods.

"Uh, OK."

I get up without looking at Ryan, because I'm sure he's staring at me with his mouth hanging open. Either that or shaking his head in disbelief.

Sadie takes my hand and leads me zigzagging through the other couples already dancing. When we stop, she wraps her arms around my neck and pulls me close. I search around for Tate to see if he's dancing with anyone. I thought he and Sadie were a couple, and I don't want to get too close if they still are. But Tate is dancing with Haley, and she's got him pulled close to her, too, so I guess it's OK. As I try to remember what Emma taught Sam about listening to the words and not worrying too much about the rhythm, I realize the song is "Stairway to Heaven." This means it's the last song of the night and the dance is almost over. I survived. I wish I could say the same about Curly's mouse.

I have my hands on Sadie's waist, and they feel like they're getting kind of clammy. I try to pull them away just a little so some air can get in. She rests her head on my shoulder. The top of her head touches my cheek. Her hair smells like bubble gum. She must have a lot of product in it, because it kind of sticks to my face. As we pivot in circles, I glance over at the couch to see what Ryan's doing, but he's gone.

Molly and Sam dance over toward us, awkwardly shuffling between couples. When they get close, Sam gives me a dorky thumbs-up. I pray no one else saw.

Where's Ryan? I mouth.

He shrugs.

When the song gets faster, I take Emma's advice and keep dancing nice and slow, but Sadie steps back a little and starts fast-dancing. I don't know what to do! I decide to try to copy her. She twirls in a circle when the song says something about winding down the road, as if she's acting out the words. I look around to see what everyone else is doing. Some people are slow-dancing and some are dancing wildly, like Sadie. I copy what she does, my face burning the whole time. I'm sure I look like an idiot. Sadie grabs my hands and starts swinging me around, laughing. She doesn't seem to care how she looks. She's just enjoying the words and the music. Pretty soon, I am too. When the song slows down again, we're both out of breath. She leans into me, and this time I don't feel awkward, even though I'm even more sweaty. She rests her head on my chest again, and I relax a little. Whoever said this is the longest song in history is right. But I'm actually kind of glad. I forget all about the mouse, and worrying about Emma, and where Ryan might be, and try to focus on this moment, because who knows if it will ever happen again?

Eventually the music stops and someone turns on the lights. The Tank barks orders to start cleaning up. I still don't see Ryan anywhere, so I help clean and figure he'll turn up eventually. When the Tank finally tells us the room is tidy enough, we all go outside to wait for our rides. Sam and I find Ryan sitting on the steps, looking crabby.

"What's wrong?" Sam asks.

"Nothing," he says, all moody. "There's your dad."

"Be right there." Sam runs off to find Molly and gives her a hug.

Ryan rolls his eyes and looks completely put out at having to wait a second longer. He is the worst when he's in a mood. *Emo,* I think. Because really.

* * *

The drive home is totally awkward. Sam talks nonstop about Molly, and his dad keeps high-fiving him in the front seat. It's so embarrassing. The whole time, Ryan stares out the window, brooding.

"So," Sam's dad asks, "did you boys dance with anyone?"

"Just once," I say.

Ryan doesn't answer.

"I think Sadie likes you," Sam announces.

Ryan moves uncomfortably in his seat, as if he just discovered he's sitting on something gross.

"Curly killed a mouse," I say, to change the subject.

Sam's dad makes a disgusted sound. "I still can't believe the school allows that cat to live there."

Now I wish I hadn't said anything.

"Curly's great," Ryan says, still staring out the window. "She's the best thing about that school."

"Molly said Lily is allergic to her," Sam says.

"Well, they'll have to get rid of her, then," Sam's dad says matter-of-factly.

"No, Dad. Lily doesn't want them to. She isn't going to tell anyone, and you can't either."

"Hmm, Sammy. I'm not sure that's a good idea."

Sam's dad talks to Sam like he's a five-year-old

whenever they disagree about something. It's so annoying. It's like if he uses that tone, it will make Sam feel little and afraid to argue.

"How can she be allergic?" Ryan asks. "Curly doesn't have any fur."

"It's not the fur," Sam says, pushing his glasses up his nose. "It's the dander."

"Dander?"

"Dandruff. Dead skin."

"Gross. I didn't know cats had that," Ryan says.

"Everyone does," Sam says, because he knows everything.

I picture Curly standing proudly with her mouse, wearing her little pink camo vest.

"They can't get rid of her," I say. "She's, like, the school mascot."

"You can't say anything, Dad. Promise!"

"OK, OK. I didn't realize you boys cared about her so much."

"We do," Sam says.

"Definitely," Ryan tells the window.

"Yes," I say. "She's the best."

* * *

At Sam's, we spread our sleeping bags out on the floor of his living room. Normally we'd stay up late talking in the dark, but as soon as Sam turns the light out, Ryan rolls over and tells us he's going to sleep.

I can't see his face, but I'm sure Sam is disappointed.

"Are you and Molly a definite thing now?" I whisper.

"Yes," he whispers happily. "Are you and Sadie?"

Ryan zips his sleeping bag up and down and makes all kinds of can't-get-comfortable noises.

"No," I say. "She didn't even talk to me."

"That doesn't mean she doesn't like you, though. Molly thinks she does. I'll tell her to ask Sadie."

"No!" I say. I wish he could see me so I could signal not to talk about it in front of Ryan.

"She's dating Tate," Ryan says from under his sleeping bag.

"Then why did she dance with Noah?"

"Because Tate was dancing with Haley."

"Why was Tate dancing with Haley?" Sam asks.

"Because Haley broke up with Big Tyler and she was sad, so Tate asked her to dance to make her feel better. But he doesn't *like*-like her. Sadie only danced with Noah because she didn't have anyone else."

"Why didn't Sadie ask to dance with Big Tyler?"

"Because the reason Haley broke up with him is that she found out he was also dating some girl from another school."

"How do you know all this?" I ask. I was with him all night. No one ever told us any of this stuff.

"I'm observant," Ryan says, as if that explains everything.

"It was a great night, wasn't it?" Sam asks dreamily.

"Yeah," Ryan says, "if you like that sort of thing."

"What sort of thing?" Sam asks.

"Hanging around at school when you don't have to be there, eating soggy chips and drinking flat soda, and listening to lame music."

"My chips weren't soggy," Sam says.

Sometimes it takes a few extra beats for Sam to get the message.

"My soda wasn't flat," I say, just to annoy Ryan.

"Whatever," he says. "It was still lame. About the only good thing that happened tonight was Curly and the mouse." He rolls over. "I'm tired."

"You're a party pooper," Sam says, disappointed. Even though he sounds like a little kid, I have to agree. Ryan is so moody—the emu.

I roll over, too, and try to get comfortable on the hard floor. As I try to sleep, I think about the mouse again, with its little paws grasping the floor, trying to crawl away. I think about how, right now, it's probably midway down Stan's neck, wrapped in snake saliva, slowly transforming into mouse juice.

The sleeping bags rustle quietly on either side of me. Then the sound of breathing steadies out. I wonder what Ryan is thinking about as he pretends to fall asleep. I wonder if he's mad at me for dancing with Sadie. Maybe I should have said no when she asked me to dance. Maybe I'm a terrible friend for leaving Ryan alone on the couch when everyone else was dancing.

I close my eyes and realize the smell I've been noticing is Sadie's perfume. I take a quiet breath and try to remember what it felt like to be so close to a girl. How it felt to have her arms around me and how fun it was to fast-dance with her, too. To act crazy and not be embarrassed. I feel like I spend half my time at school worrying if I have anything in my teeth or if I smell. Or if my hair looks dumb or if anyone can tell I'm wearing "husky" jeans. I'm always worried about screwing something up. For just that one minute tonight, nothing mattered. It was just the music and me moving to it the way it told me to.

Ryan and Sam are both snoring steadily now. I breathe again, smelling that smell that will always remind me of "Stairway to Heaven," that dance, and Sadie, smiling at me.

7

We Are Too Old for Picture Day

Ryan is still moody in the morning. Before we even get out of our sleeping bags, he tells us he has to go home right after breakfast because he has a lot of homework. Usually we lounge around for a while and play video games before we stuff our faces with whatever food we can find in Sam's cupboards. We make weird bagel toppings and see who can come up with the best names for them. But today, we just have boring old cream cheese. I love visiting Sam and Ryan, because Emma isn't around to yell at me for eating stuff I'm not "supposed" to. I don't remind Ryan about his vegan promise to Emma, since I'm sure that would only make his foul mood worse.

"Good luck with that homework," I tell him when his mom comes to pick him up.

He nods and doesn't even say thanks to Sam's parents.

To be honest, it's kind of a relief to see him go.

"We have *got* to find him a girlfriend," Sam says as we roll up the sleeping bags.

"Definitely."

I follow him to his bedroom, where he opens his closet and starts pulling out some button-up shirts on hangers. "What are you wearing for Picture Day on Monday? I can't decide."

"I wasn't really planning on anything special," I say.

"Well, you should. They put our pictures on our student IDs. You'll be stuck with it all year, so you better try to look good."

"No one looks at our IDs, do they? What do we even need them for?"

"Museum discounts."

I roll my eyes.

Sam sets out a bunch of shirts on his bed, then steps back and studies them.

"I hate Picture Day," I tell him. "This is middle school. Aren't we too old for this?"

He ignores me and picks up an orange plaid shirt and holds it under his chin in front of the mirror. "You need to embrace the inevitable, Noah. Picture Day is happening. Make sure you look good for it."

At school on Monday morning, everything feels off. Half the boys have overcombed their hair, so it looks like their moms did it. Most of the girls show up with extra makeup, stiffly sprayed hair, and too much perfume. I don't know why they wear perfume, since you can't smell it in the picture. I guess it's all just part of the getting-dressed-up package.

When Jem Thomas walks in, everyone stops and stares. He's wearing a sweatshirt and black dress pants. Normally he has pretty messy bedhead hair, but today it's plastered against his skull and he has a part. I know Emma would say it's sexist of me, but I really don't think guys should have parts. Jem looks miserable. After an awkward moment of silence, we all go back to worrying about our own weird hair.

The Tank ushers us down the hall where the photographers are waiting. There's a big screen against the wall and a light with one of those umbrellas to help with the glare. We line up in the hallway and take turns peering toward the front. A lady with long blond hair walks up and down the line, inspecting us.

"Do you want a comb?" she asks me.

I blush. I don't know why I get embarrassed when strangers talk to me.

"No, thank you. I'm OK," I mumble.

"I think you want a comb," she says, handing me one anyway. It's one of those cheap tiny black combs that are basically useless. I don't even know why they exist. Maybe solely for Picture Day.

I turn to Ryan, who's standing behind me. "Do I need this?" I ask, holding up the comb.

He shrugs. "You look fine." But he doesn't even check when he says it.

Ryan has been acting weird toward me all morning.

I nudge Sam. "*Do* I?"

He squints at me for a minute and pushes his glasses up his nose. "No. Don't change it."

I don't know why I trust Sam, whose hair is still wet and combed flat on the top of his head just as strangely as Jem's. But at least he put some effort into making sure all is well.

I lean against the wall and sigh. Why don't parents want their kids to look like they normally do in pictures? Why do they want them to look like some scary miniature businessmen instead?

Molly stands behind Sam in line. They're holding hands. I think Ryan sees at the same time I do. He makes this huffy breathing noise, like holding hands is the most obnoxious thing two people could do. Ever. For someone who was so relieved to escape Molly, he looks kind of dejected. Personally, I think he did the right thing. Molly is definitely not his type. I wonder if there is a girl version of emo. Ryan needs an emo-ette.

As we inch closer, we can see the photographer and his assistant make each person stand on this taped square on a pad in front of the photographer. When it's Jem's turn, he hesitates.

"Are you taking off your sweatshirt, hon?" the hair lady asks.

He takes a deep breath. "Yeah," he says. He looks out at the rest of us kind of apologetically, as if what we're about to see is going to be horrifying. Then he slowly pulls off his sweatshirt. The shirt underneath is white with black cuffs at the wrist. The collar is also black but has gold on the tips. Everyone cranes their necks to look more closely.

"I heard his parents make him wear crazy stuff for Picture Day, and man, they weren't exaggerating," Ryan whispers.

"Can you hurry, please?" Jem asks the woman. She fidgets with his collar and makes a disapproving face. Jem cringes. I've never seen anyone look so miserable. Not even Ryan.

"Just trying to straighten you out a little, hon," she says. She fidgets with his shoulders, which also have some sort of extra black material. "I didn't know they still made shirts with epaulets."

"What are epaulets?" I ask.

"They don't need to be straight," Jem says. "Please. Just take the picture."

"Epaulets are those funny things on his shoulders," Sam whispers loudly. "Usually they're on military uniforms. With tassels."

"Tassels?" Ryan asks. "Wow, I was thinking it couldn't possibly get worse, but I guess it could. Jem lucked out."

The woman fidgets with one of the black stripes

on Jem's shoulder, then shrugs and steps back. "Suit yourself, but you know if your parents don't like how these come out, you'll have to do this all over again when we come back on Makeup Day."

Jem groans and shifts his shoulders a little. As soon as the photographer takes a photo, he puts his sweat-shirt back on and rushes past all of us.

Someone mumbles, "Ahoy there, sailor!" and a bunch of people crack up, but not really in a mean way. Jem just keeps on walking.

"Next!" the photographer yells.

We inch closer until it's my turn. The woman takes my form and then shows me where to stand.

"Put your hands in your pockets," she tells me.

"Huh?"

"You're getting a waist-up photo, so you need to have a different pose."

"Are you sure?" I ask.

"That's what's checked off on the form," she says. "Half-body, rainbow background."

Ryan snorts.

I roll my eyes. "My sister must have filled that out as a joke," I say.

"What's so funny?" the lady asks, all offended.

"Nuh-nothing," I say. "I'm just sure my parents would want the normal one."

"Well, it says here they don't, and I have to go by what's on the form."

I put my hands in my pockets.

"Not like that," she says. "Take your thumb out, like this." She models for me.

Ryan snickers.

"Shoulders back. Tilt your head. No, the other way."

I try to move the way she says but feel like an idiot.

"Smile! Smile!"

I try to smile.

Sam and Ryan start laughing.

"Open your mouth a little. People never realize how silly they look when they smile with their mouths closed."

I wish *she* would try closing her mouth for five seconds.

I open my mouth a little and try to grin naturally. It feels weird.

"It'll have to do," the woman says. I think she takes her job a little too seriously.

The camera clicks, and I step away to join Jem in the after-picture hall of shame. It's crowded, which makes me feel better about the whole thing.

At home that night, Emma asks me all about Picture Day. I tell her I don't think her prank was very funny.

"What?" she asks, all surprised. "I thought that would crack you up!"

"It might have if it *wasn't me*," I say.

"How selfish." She punches me in the arm the way she does.

"You're not funny," I repeat.

She grins. "How'd you like your Tofurky sandwich?" she asks me.

"It was gross," I say. "And that wasn't mayonnaise, either."

"I know. It was Vegenaise. Yummy and kind to animals."

I'm starting to think maybe I should trade breakfast responsibility with lunch after all. Only, I know my mom would flip if I suggested we change our routine. God forbid anyone try to tell Emma what to eat.

"If you're going to insist on making me a vegan,

then just give me vegetables or something, OK? Fake meat is such an insult."

"To who?"

"To meat!"

"Meat doesn't have feelings."

"Just stick with peanut butter and jelly, OK?"

"All right," she says. Then she punches me in the arm one more time before going off to make our lunches for tomorrow. I wish she wouldn't make them the night before. By the time I get around to eating my lunch the next day, the bread is either soggy or stale, depending on what's inside. The other thing she puts in there are these energy bars that are supposed to taste like chocolate but taste like something vaguely of chocolate essence and more like sawdust. Not that I've ever eaten sawdust, but that's what I imagine it would taste like if I ever decided to try.

I start my homework but get interrupted by Sam texting me about Sadie. He said he caught her watching me and smiling during my fashion shoot.

Fashion shoot. That's just great.

I'm tempted to go yell at Emma again for ruining my life, because I get this feeling that by tomorrow when I get back to school, I'm going to have some kind of new embarrassing nickname that has something to do with either rainbows or a male model.

I text Sam back to tell him it wasn't a fashion shoot and then turn off my phone so he can't argue with me or make me feel any worse.

The Captain jumps up on my bed and circles until he makes a nice nest to curl up in.

I flop down next to him and stare at the ceiling until I hear a distinct whistle slip out of his butt and my room turns toxic.

"Emma!" I yell. "Stop feeding the dog Tofurky! You're going to kill us all!"

The Captain wags his tail, which only spreads the smell even more.

We're the kind of family that always sits at the same place at the table. My mom and dad on the ends, me and Emma across from each other in the middle.

Tonight we're having roasted potatoes, broccoli, baked tofu smothered in barbecue sauce, and bread made by my dad. My dad loves to make bread. He also loves to cook, though since Emma started making all her vegan demands, I think he likes it less. My dad is the kind of cook who roasts or smokes some sort of meat all day long and makes everyone comment on how much more amazing it is because of all that waiting and smoking when really none of us can tell the difference. For a while, it was only Emma who was vegan. But she kept adding these crazy rules about how my dad cooked. Like if he grilled meat and vegetables, the vegetables couldn't be grilled where the meat touched. Then she wouldn't even eat the vegetables if they'd been on the same grill at all. Normal parents would just put their foot down and say, "Too bad—you'll eat what we tell you!" But not in our house. When it comes to food, my parents will do anything if it means Emma eats a healthy diet.

So, my dad's stuck with figuring out creative ways to make tofu taste like something other than sponge.

I take a bite of tofu and try to swallow it as quickly as possible.

"I think I really got it this time," my dad says. He gives me a hopeful look.

I swallow a huge swig of water. "Great sauce, Dad."

"Yeah," Emma agrees, though I notice she hasn't actually brought any of the food to her mouth.

"You think?" he asks, all excited.

She cuts a tofu cube with the edge of her fork and moves a piece away from the rest, forming a barbecue trail across her plate. Then she does the same with a piece of potato and broccoli. She does this all very slowly and methodically and then asks my dad something about a tofu press and whether he would like one.

He beams and starts telling her how he can make his own using a heavy pot, and while he's explaining it, he seems to forget all about waiting for her to actually try a bite.

My mom keeps eyeing Emma's plate. She's always eyeing Emma's plate. "Emma, you've haven't tried anything yet," she points out.

"Yes, I have," Emma says. "It's delicious, Dad."

"You're just moving your food around," my mom says cautiously.

My dad gives her a warning look.

"I tried it, *Mom*," Emma says. She deliberately picks up a piece of tofu with her fork and eats it.

"Thank you," my mom says.

"Jem's parents made him wear a horrible shirt for Picture Day," I say, to change the subject. "It had epaulets. People didn't make too much fun of him, though, because I think it was so over-the-top embarrassing, he passed humiliation and went straight to sympathy."

"It's such a good school," my mom says. "The kids are so kind to each other."

Emma snorts.

"It is!" my mom insists.

Emma drinks from her water glass. I wonder if she's having *Lord of the Flies* list memories.

"I don't think I let the tofu marinate long enough," my dad says.

"It's great, Dad, really," Emma tells him. But I notice she hasn't taken another bite.

Later, when Emma pops her head into my room to say good night, I ask her if she's OK.

"Not you, too," she says, all annoyed. "I'm fine. I just didn't like what dad did with the tofu and didn't want to say anything to hurt his feelings. Everyone needs to relax!"

"You could have had something else," I say.

"Honestly, Noah, you are really annoying sometimes."

"Excuse me for caring," I say.

Instead of fighting back, she turns and leaves me in the dark. The Captain gets up and goes after her, but she slams her door before he can follow her into her room, so he comes back and settles on my floor again.

"What's her problem?" I ask him. But I'm not sure I really want to know.

8

The Fart Squad
Needs to Be
Disbanded

On our last day using the potter's wheel in art class, I turn the wheel and gently reach my fingers into the ball of soft clay, shaping it slowly and carefully. Like magic, the ridges of my bowl begin to rise up, and I ease my fingers to widen the ridge.

Ms. Cliff watches intensely. "Thaaaaaat's it," she says. "Not too fast."

I press my thumbs deeper and the sides form upward, just the way I imagined. It's as if I only have to picture the bowl in my head the way I want it to form, and somehow my hands make the clay grow into that shape. When I have the curves and form just right, I let the wheel spin down and slowly move my fingers away.

"Beautiful," Ms. Cliff says. "Just gorgeous, Noah. You have a real gift."

She helps me move the bowl to the next station and then wanders off to help Sadie, who's waiting in line.

"Nice bowl," Ryan says. He's holding his own bowl, cupped in his hands. One side has fallen in on itself. "I think I'll give this to my dad's new girlfriend for Christmas," he says.

"What is it?"

"It's a symbolic work of art. Can't you tell? The caved-in side represents"—he thinks for a minute—"what she's done to my life."

"I'm sure she'll appreciate that."

"I don't want her to appreciate it. I want her to feel my pain and know she's the cause of it."

"I didn't know you were in pain."

"I'm in agony."

"You hide it well."

"Agony comes in different shapes and sizes."

"Why are you in agony? What did your dad's girl-friend ever do to you?"

"As long as she's in the picture, my parents will

never get back together." He pokes the indent so it sags even more.

"You can fix that, you know," I say.

"Why would I want to fix it?"

I give up.

"She's the reason I'm an emu," he tells me. "If it weren't for her, I could be your average, cheerful all-American kid. Instead"—he gestures to his dark clothes and makes a mopey face—"this."

"*Emo,*" I correct him. "And I don't think if you call yourself that, you really are."

"What do you know?" he says.

We put our bowls on the tray with the other bowls waiting to be glazed or fired, then walk over to Curly, who is sunning herself on the dry shelf in front of the window.

"How many mice do you think she actually kills every day?" Ryan asks.

"I don't know. Hopefully not more than one. Isn't that what the Tank said?"

"Still. That adds up to three hundred and sixty-five murders a year. Minimum."

"It's a lot."

"Especially for someone so puny."

She looks up at us and purrs, asking for a pat. But I can't bring myself to touch her weird skin, so I just kind of gently rub her back through her vest. Today's is blue with a gray Totoro on the back, smiling up at me.

"Class is over," Ms. Cliff sort of sings. "Make sure you put everything you leave out of Curly's reach!"

I follow Ryan out to the hall and nearly plow into him as soon as we step outside, because he has stopped in his tracks.

"What. Is. That?" he asks.

I look. Sam and Molly appear to be making out at Sam's locker. We step closer, and sure enough, that is exactly what we see. They seem totally oblivious of the growing crowd entering the hall.

"Unbelievable," Ryan says. "Sam gets his first kiss before us?"

"I didn't know it was a competition," I say.

As we walk by, Ryan bumps into Sam. "Get a room," he says.

"Hey!" Sam wipes his mouth. His lips are bright red. So are his cheeks.

Molly stares at him like he's a super stud. "See you later," she says, then kisses him on the cheek.

Ryan shakes his head and opens his locker in disgust.

"What?" Sam asks.

"You," Ryan says. He grabs a book and slams his locker.

"Huh?"

Instead of answering, Ryan storms down the hall.

"Boy," Sam says, "I never thought Ryan would be the jealous type."

We watch Ryan turn the corner at the end of the hall and go into Madame Estelle's room, then bolt back out, covering his mouth and nose. "Stupid Fart Squad!" he yells. He kicks a locker door and storms away.

"Wow. He used to want to be a member," Sam says, grabbing his French book. "He's been acting weird ever since I started dating Molly."

I don't deny it.

"We need to find someone for him before he drives me crazy."

"But who?" I ask.

"I'm not sure. Sadie? I know he has a crush on her."

My heart sinks.

"No offense or anything," he says. "I know you probably kind of like her. But I think if anything was going to happen with the two of you, it would have. That ship has sailed. You really blew your chance at the dance, Noah."

"I thought she was dating Tate. Why would I have made a move at the dance?"

"They have an open relationship," Sam says, acting all sophisticated.

"What the heck does that mean?"

He pushes his glasses up his nose. "They can date other people."

"Why would they do that?" I ask.

"How should I know?" he says, suddenly sounding like his old self. "Molly told me they're more like friends who want to date someone but haven't found anyone else, so they stay together, even though they don't really like each other as more than friends."

"That's dumb."

"Well, we're all dumb," Sam says. "In one way or another."

"How are you dumb?"

"I don't know. I just am." He smiles and leans his head toward me. "Molly thinks I'm a good kisser," he whispers.

I pull my head away. "I can't believe you kissed

her with that breath," I say, waving my hand in front of my face.

"What?" He breathes into the cup of his hand and blows, then sniffs. "I don't smell anything."

"You can't smell your own breath, dummy."

"What does it smell like?"

"Onions."

He nods. "Molly shared her salad with me."

"What is it with you two and smelly food?"

He rifles through his bag and pulls out a tin. "Mints!"

"Terrific," I say. "You might want to share them with Molly."

"I will," he says gleefully. "And then we'll make out again."

"Good for you." I'm tempted to storm down the hall like Ryan at this point, but I don't. "Just don't do it in front of me. And especially not Ryan."

"Fine. Hey, do you really like Sadie? Or have you given up? Seriously."

"I don't know," I say. "Maybe both."

"Well, decide," he says. "Because Molly and I need someone to double-date with, and I can't stand Tate."

"That's generous."

"You know what I mean. C'mon. Ask her out."

"I don't think so," I say.

He shakes his head. "Sheesh. I never thought I'd be the one with a girlfriend and you and Ryan would be the ones left alone."

"Whatever," I say.

I'm starting to get why Ryan has been so moody.

In French, Madame Estelle makes us repeat after her, *"Elle est petite. Il est petit. Nous sommes petits."* Ryan ignores us by pretending to pay attention and be a good student. He says the phrases extra loud, with a French-accent flair. Madame Estelle beams at him. It's so annoying.

I say the words quietly because I hate my accent. Sam bellows out the words in an exaggerated way, which makes him sound more like a loud Texan than a Parisian.

"Bon! Bon!" Madame Estelle keeps saying, though, like she doesn't mind. *"Qui peut me donner un exemple de quelque chose de petit?"* Madame asks.

An example of something small? Hm. I don't know. This is when Ryan's *Who's to say?* trick could possibly come in handy.

Lily pipes up. *"Curly est petite!"*

"Oui! Quoi d'autre?"

"Noah's tête est petite," Ryan says.

"What?" I say.

"Monsieur Ryan," Madame says, *"qu'est-ce que vous avez dit?"*

"Uhhhh," Ryan stammers. *"La tête de Noah est petite?"*

He points to my head, and everyone looks at me.

"It is!" Sam says, and starts laughing. The class joins in, including Sadie.

"En français!" Madame demands.

I give Ryan a dirty look, but he just grins.

I would like to say Ryan is a small emu, but I don't know the words *en français*. Why can't every class be as easy as art?

9
The Storage Shed Is Not for Kissing Behind

After school, we sit on the steps and wait for our rides. Tate and Sadie come out and disappear behind the storage unit, where the school keeps the outdoor gym equipment. Miranda and Belle follow, then Molly and Sam. Before Sam goes behind the building, he looks back at us and waves.

"What do you think they do back there?" I ask Ryan.

"What do you *think*?" he answers sarcastically.

I picture them all making out. "That's not very romantic," I say.

"Well, where else are they gonna go?" he asks.

"Good point."

We both sigh at the same time and watch the shed.

"Has anyone seen Curly?" the Tank calls from behind us. "I can't find her. I hope she didn't get out. No one let her out, right?"

If anyone did, no one admits it.

Ryan and I jump up. "We'll find her," Ryan says.

Lily follows us inside. We wander through the classrooms and call her name.

"Here, kitty, kitty," Lily sings.

"Cur-ly!" I call encouragingly. "Want a treat?"

"You don't have a treat," Ryan says.

"She doesn't know that. It's how we get the Captain to come when we want him."

"That's mean."

"She's happy with a pat. Don't worry about it."

"She'll never trust you again."

"I'll risk it."

We call and call, but there's no sign of her. The longer we look, the more I get that helpless feeling again. What if she got outside? How will she survive in the cold with just her measly vest?

After searching all the classrooms, we go to the

Community Room and look under the couches and in the closets but can't find her there, either.

"What if she ran away?" Lily asks. "Would she do that?"

"Why would she leave such a good situation?" Ryan asks. "Plenty of clothes. Mice. Always a lap to sit on? It doesn't make sense."

"Curly!" I call out again. "Curly, come get a treat!"

Something in the ceiling scratches.

"Curly?" Lily says.

Scratch.

"Curly! Is that you?" I ask.

Scritch-scratch.

"She's stuck in the ceiling! Mr. Sticht! We found her!" Lily yells.

Ryan and I drag a table under the part of the ceiling where we heard the scratching, then climb up. The ceiling is made up of a bunch of square-shaped pieces that you can push up and move, so we start pushing a bunch, careful to avoid touching the wads of gum some student from the past pelted up here, until I can feel the weight of Curly on one. "Here!" I say to Ryan, pointing to the next square.

"Careful, boys," the Tank says when he comes bounding into the room.

Ryan slowly pushes the square next to the one Curly is on up and over, leaving a big hole in the ceiling.

Curly peeks out and mews pitifully.

"C'mon, girl," Ryan says.

"Treat," I add.

Curly mews again and pokes a paw out.

Ryan reaches up for her and pulls her down. "She's shaking!"

"Give her to me," Lily says, holding out her hands.

"But you're allerg—"

"I'll take her," I say, interrupting Ryan before he can spill the beans and get Curly kicked out.

I jump down from the table and reach up for Curly. She has a cobweb hanging from one ear. I wipe it off and then hold her against my chest. She starts to purr.

"Poor thing," the Tank says. "Curly, what on earth were you doing up there?"

"Maybe there was a mouse," Lily says.

"In the ceiling?" Ryan asks. "Gross!"

"Mice are everywhere," Lily says matter-of-factly.

"I'm just glad we found her," the Tank says. "You had us worried sick, girl!"

"How do you think she got up in there?" I ask.

"Who knows? It's an old building. There are holes all over the place. I'll have Ms. Leonard take a look." Ms. Leonard is the school janitor.

"You guys should probably go back out. Your rides might be here."

"Be good," I say, setting Curly on the floor. She shakes herself like a wet dog, then walks over to the Tank and rubs against his legs.

"Crazy cat," he says. There's a catch in his voice, as if he got choked up.

Lily hooks her arms through mine and Ryan's. "My heroes," she says. It's embarrassing, but also feels kind of nice. I look over at Ryan, who has a huge grin on his face. Too bad Lily is dating the pole dancer.

As we climb the stairs, Sam and Molly start toward us. "What happened?" Sam asks. Their cheeks are bright red, which, according to Sam, means that they've been kissing a long time.

"My heroes saved Curly," Lily says, letting go of our arms. "She got stuck in the ceiling, but they got her out safe and sound."

Sam looks impressed. We all go back out and sit on the steps. Molly sits on the one below Sam and leans back against his legs.

Ryan takes one look at them and rolls his eyes so hard, I think they'll get stuck up there. "Get a room," he says, annoyed. It's his new phrase whenever they so much as hold hands.

They ignore him.

"Noah!" Emma yells from the passenger side of our car as my mom pulls forward. "C'mon!"

"Hey, Emma," Ryan calls to her.

Emma waves and gives him her "I'm so cute, of course you have a crush on me" smile.

"See you guys tomorrow," I say.

Lily stands up when I do and gives me a hug. "Thanks for saving Curly."

"Um, no problem," I say awkwardly.

"Hey, how come you didn't hug me?" Ryan asks.

"I was waiting to hug you good-bye. Stand up and I'll hug you now if you want."

Ryan jumps up, and Lily throws her arms around him. He smiles at me over her shoulder.

"Get a room," I say.

"Ha, ha."

* * *

"That was a nice hug," Emma says when I get into the car.

"Is everything OK, honey?" my mom asks. "Why was Lily consoling you?"

"She wasn't consoling me—she was thanking me for helping Curly get unstuck from the ceiling."

"Stupid cat," Stu says.

"She was probably trying to catch a mouse or something. She's not stupid."

"They need to find a more humane way of keeping the mouse population down," Emma says. "They should get some have-a-heart traps. If all the parents knew about Curly's real purpose, they'd have a fit."

"What do you mean her real purpose?" my mom asks.

"She's the school assassin," Emma says.

"No, she's not!" Harper says. "She's the school therapy pet."

"She's both," I say. "And don't tell anyone, Harper, or you could get her in trouble."

"I don't know about this . . ." my mom says.

"What's there to know?" I ask. "Why is everyone so against Curly?"

"She *kills* things," Emma says.

"It's not very hygienic," my mom adds.

"What if she gets rabies?" Harper asks.

"You can't get rabies from mice," I say.

"How do you know?" Emma asks.

"Have you ever heard of a rabid mouse?"

"That doesn't mean they don't exist."

"You seem awfully attached to that cat," my mom says.

"She's a good cat—that's all. You guys are over-reacting."

After we drop off Harper and Stu, Emma turns around in her seat to talk again.

"Sadie's older sister told me she thinks Sadie has a crush on you."

"She has a boyfriend," I point out.

Emma shrugs.

"Sadie is so cute!" my mom says. "I love her hair."

"She has a boyfriend," I point out again.

"Apparently that's just for convenience."

"She was making out with him behind the storage shed. That doesn't seem like convenience."

"Where were the teachers when this was happening?" my mom asks.

"Never mind," I say.

"Maybe she just kisses him for fun," Emma says, ignoring my mom. "It doesn't mean she likes him."

"Really, Emma," my mom says. "I doubt Sadie is like that."

"Like what?"

"You know what I mean," my mom says.

Emma turns back around to face my mom. "No, I don't, Mom. Why don't you explain?"

"Can we stop talking about this now?" I ask. I can tell by the tone of her voice that Emma is about to get preachy about girls and double standards.

I see my mom purse her lips in the mirror, as if she's forcing herself to stop talking in order to avoid a fight with Emma. It seems like the two of them are at each other more and more lately.

Emma deliberately shifts her body away from my mom and stares out the window.

We drive the rest of the way home in silence.

As soon as I get my homework spread out on my desk, Ryan texts me.

RYAN: I think Lily likes me

ME: Great

RYAN: No really

ME: Great!

RYAN: Why can't you get excited?

ME: Great!!!!!!!!!!!!!!!!!!!!!

RYAN:

ME: Do you like her?

RYAN: I don't know.

I call him.

"Why are you so excited that Lily likes you if you don't even know if you like her?" I ask.

"It's just nice that someone finally likes me, I guess."

"Someone *did* like you, remember? Molly? And you hid from her for days. I can't get those hours of my life I wasted with you in the bathroom back, you know."

"It wasn't *hours*."

"Any time spent in the bathroom is multiplied by seven. It's like dog years. Only a million times worse, because they are *horrible* years."

"Fine. Sorry."

"So, are you going to hide from Lily or go after

her? You are aware that she's actually dating the pole dancer. Right?"

"Well, yeah. But that's not gonna last. She just said yes to him because she had fun at the dance with him. He mostly disgusts her. She just forgot."

"Why do you sound so miserable again?"

He's quiet. "Am I shallow?"

"No. You're emu."

"E*mo*."

"Right. That."

"I don't actually think I am anymore. I've discovered I'm not really all that sensitive."

"I've noticed," I say. "But at least you're nice to Curly."

"She seems to be the only person who doesn't annoy me lately."

"Except that she's not a person."

"Ugh. I know! That's probably why. Can you imagine if she was a person? She'd be awesome."

"Except a human who catches mice with her teeth and claws and then tortures them before killing and eating them would be pretty creepy and gross."

"True. And a human would look really stupid in those vests."

"Do you think cats can get rabies from killing mice?"

"Do mice get rabies?" Ryan asks. "I've never heard of a rabid mouse, but a little mouse zombie frothing at the mouth would be amazing. That would make the best movie ever."

I move over to my bed and lie down. Up on my ceiling, there are little gray marks from the time Ryan, Sam, and I bounced a Super Ball off the wall and tried to catch it from our sleeping bags. I think we were eight or so. That was a fun night, until my mom came up to check on us and had a fit. She told me we were going to have to paint the ceiling as punishment. We were all set to do it the next weekend, too. But the next weekend is when the Thing We Don't Talk About happened, and my mom forgot all about the ceiling. And for a while, all about me.

"Hey," I say. "I need to get back to my homework."

"OK. See you tomorrow."

I hang up and stare at the ceiling again. In the next room, I can hear Emma's music playing just loud enough to be annoying but not loud enough for my mom to make her turn it down.

Emma is into old songs that were popular a long

time ago. Songs by the Smiths, the Cure, the Clash, and a bunch of other bands I don't really know. It's all a little angry and a little pumped-up and a little sad. She's so serious about everything she does. Like it all has to have a *purpose*. Even her music inspires her to be a certain way, like angry or pumped-up or sad. She gets so into the things she listens to and reads, but I think sometimes they make her do crazy things, like making the *Lord of the Flies* list. And whenever I hear certain songs she's playing, I know what mood she'll be in. Lately she's been listening to a lot of angry stuff. I can tell it's putting her in a bad mood. I can also tell that it has my parents worried, even though no one really talks about it. No one talks about anything around here, except my parents when they think I can't hear them. They're always talking in worried whispers that get too loud the angrier and more worried they get. Lately, they seem to be getting worse.

I pat my bed and let the Captain jump up. He licks my arm and makes a happy slobber sound. Sometimes I think the Captain is the only one in this family who remembers that I need some attention once in a while, too. He says "You're welcome" by letting off a doozy. Sometimes I really can't win.

10

Prevent Locker Juice: DO NOT Leave Food in Your Locker Over Break

On the last day of school before Thanksgiving, the Tank makes us clean out our lockers. Small Tyler wanders around helping everyone else, because ever since the Locker Juice Incident, he's refused to use his locker and carries everything he needs in his backpack. As a joke, someone put an official-looking notice on his locker door that says HAZARDOUS MATERIALS, and it hasn't been opened since.

Curly wanders the halls, pouncing on crumpled-up balls of paper. She's wearing a vest with turkeys on it.

"What happens to Curly during break?" I ask Lily, who knows everything.

"She's going home with Ms. Cliff," Lily says. She sneezes.

"Are you really allergic?" I whisper.

"Don't bring it up," she whispers back. She bends down to pet Curly.

It's funny: I never really thought of Lily as the kind of person who would be protective of a skinny little cat, especially after what happened to the mouse. I guess it just goes to show that you can think you know someone, and then they do something totally unexpected and everything changes. Part of me really hopes she breaks up with Zach and asks Ryan out.

Sam and I finish up pretty fast, so we offer to help Ryan. At first he acts all grouchy toward us, which is getting tiring. Then Sadie and Tate walk down the hall holding hands, and Sadie says hi to me but not to Sam or Ryan.

"You should definitely ask her out," Sam says. "She obviously likes you."

"Did you not notice the hand-holding?" I ask.

"I already explained that."

"But it made no sense."

Ryan slams his locker hard. "This school is ridiculous. No one is going out with who they really want to."

"I am," Sam says.

"You don't count."

"What's that supposed to mean?"

"Just forget it," Ryan says. "Whatever."

We go outside and sit on the steps.

"What are you guys doing over break?" Sam asks us.

Ryan shrugs. "I have to go to my grandparents' with my dad. My mom's all upset about it, but my dad says she gets me for Christmas vacation, so she has nothing to complain about. They treat me like some kind of decoration they each think looks better at their house."

"I thought you were Jewish," Sam says.

"Only half. My mom's Jewish and my dad's an ex-Catholic. He calls our winter break Christmas vacation just to annoy my mom."

"It still sounds better than my vacation," Sam says. "My parents invited my grandparents to stay with us, and I have to give up my room for three days. My grandpa is really old and forgets where he is half the time and says stuff like, 'Ella'—that's my grandmother's name—'who is that boy at the end of the table?' And then my grandmother will start to cry and then my mom will start to cry and he'll say, 'Ella, why is everyone crying? Did someone die?' And my mom and grandmother will just cry harder, because it's kind of like my grandfather is the one who died, even though he's still alive."

"Jeez," Ryan says. He picks up a pebble off the step and tosses it. It bumps down the steps and disappears. "Please tell me your vacation is better than ours, Noah."

"Not really. Emma will probably make some kind of scary tofu mold in the shape of a turkey that no one will eat, and then fight with my parents about whether they can offer guests real food, like actual turkey and gravy."

"Emma sure is intense," Sam says.

"That's one way to describe it."

Ryan elbows Sam to be quiet, since they both know Emma is more than intense.

"Molly invited me to her house, but my parents won't let me go," Sam says. "They say it's not normal for a middle-school kid to spend a holiday with his girlfriend."

"Well, yeah," Ryan says. "I mean, you just started going out. You're not exactly engaged."

"It feels like a long time for middle school," Sam says.

"Middle-school time is like dog-year time," I point out. "You've got to multiply it by seven."

"This doesn't count," Ryan says. "That only applies to misery."

"I'm glad you don't think I'm in misery," Sam says. "Because I am actually very happy."

Ryan just gives him a look.

"Are dogs in misery?" I ask.

"No, they just age really fast, which is sad," Ryan explains.

Ryan has become a little too good at being a downer.

On Thanksgiving morning, Emma and my dad are busy in the kitchen making preparations for dinner. My parents invited Ryan's mom, since she's alone for the holiday. It's going to be weird having her here without Ryan. They also invited Emma's friend Sara and her parents. And the new couple who moved in a few houses down, Mark and Mitch. My parents are obsessed with making sure no one they know is alone during the holidays. My mom is all stressed-out, though, because Emma freaked when my dad said he thought we should serve a real turkey. But my dad put his foot down and said since we are having guests, we had to serve a traditional meal along with her vegan one. When I go into the kitchen, I can tell Emma is still upset, because she's chopping vegetables with a vengeance and every time my dad opens the oven to baste the turkey, she runs out of the room, saying the smell is making her sick.

I have nowhere to go but escape to my room with the Captain, who hates it when Emma gets angry. I wonder if his dog-years ratio is even worse because of all the stress around here.

I stare up at the Super-Ball marks on the ceiling and wish Sam and Ryan were here, even if they do bicker too much. At least it's not over food.

I scroll through my last set of messages I got from Sam and think about writing back but don't. It's all Molly, Molly, Molly, and I have no advice. He's already stressing about what to get her for Christmas! I hope he's not sending stuff like this to Ryan, because I don't know how much more of this lovey-dovey stuff Ryan can take before he snaps.

I decide to text Ryan and see how he's doing with his dad, but I get a DELIVERY FAILED message.

The first guest to arrive is Ryan's mom. She's about twenty minutes early, and my dad and Emma are still busy making last-minute dishes, so my mom and I keep her company. She looks pretty miserable. In fact, I don't really think I've seen her look happy since she and Ryan's dad got divorced last year. The whole story is pretty terrible. She supposedly fell in love with her hair stylist and told Ryan's dad. His dad flipped out and got really depressed. They tried therapy to save their marriage, but it didn't work. It's too bad, because it turns out his mom didn't even have an affair with the hair stylist. She just loved him. Or the idea of him. He was nice to her and talked to her and seemed to listen as if he cared, which, according to my mom, is what all stylists do to get big tips. Ryan says his mom just loved the *idea* of her stylist. She didn't really love *him*. But by the time she figured that out, Ryan's dad had moved out and gotten a new girlfriend. So after telling her husband she liked someone else because he paid attention to her, she ended up feeling even more alone than she was before.

This kind of explains why Ryan gets bitter around happy couples.

"I wish Ryan was here," she says sadly.

My mom pats her knee. "Would you like a drink? I make a mean Bloody Mary."

"Oh, that sounds perfect," she says, putting her hand on my mom's. "Thanks, Louise."

"You got it." My mom rushes off to make the drink and leaves us alone.

Mrs. Lamper is wearing an off-white shiny blouse that seems to be missing a button. I wish I hadn't noticed that, but when she leaned forward, her shirt sort of bulged open and her bra showed, and now I can't unsee it.

She fidgets with a long gold necklace and smiles awkwardly. "It was nice of your parents to invite me," she says. She leans forward to take a nut from the dish on the coffee table.

I quickly look away as the missing-button space gapes open again.

She sits back and eats an almond.

This is probably the longest five minutes of my life so far.

"Have you heard from Ryan?" she asks when she finishes chewing.

"No," I say.

She looks disappointed.

"Sam?"

I shake my head.

"They don't seem to be getting along too well. Do you know what that's about?"

She starts to bend forward for another nut.

"I'll go see what's taking my mom so long," I say. How long does it take to make a stupid drink, anyway?

Emma and my dad are busy putting dishes together while my mom pours vegetable juice into a glass. "How much vodka do I add, Jeff? I can't remember."

"Depends on who it's for," my dad says.

"That's not funny," she says, smiling. She dumps some vodka in and stirs it with a celery stick. "I need to get back out there and keep her company. Noah, can you help put food out? The hot plates are all plugged in on the buffet. You just need to set things on it. I want everything to be ready so we can enjoy cocktails with our guests before dinner."

Emma hands me a plate of mashed potatoes to bring out. "Come back for the squash, OK? And please put all my dishes on one end of the sideboard and Dad's meat ones on the other." She says "meat" in this exaggerated way, like she really means maggots or something equally offensive.

I go back and forth for all Emma's dishes. There's squash, green beans with slivered almonds, tiny pumpkins filled with soup, cauliflower with fake cheese melted on top, dinner rolls, and, of course, a seitan turkey, which smells nothing like turkey and doesn't really look like one, either. In fact, it smells like what you might imagine hell to smell like, so that's appropriate. The gravy Emma made smells suspicious, too.

My dad's dishes, on the other hand, smell amazing. It's been so long since I ate meat, I kind of forgot how good it smelled. I'm tempted to sneak a bunch of the stuffing made with turkey broth, but if Emma saw me, I know she'd be upset. I wonder if my parents will eat it or just offer it to the guests.

While people start to arrive, I see Emma go into the

dining room and put little paper signs in front of each dish. I wander over to see if she wants help. In front of my dad's roasted turkey, she's put a little paper taped to a toothpick that says CONTAINS DEATH.

"Seriously?" I ask.

She gives me a look.

"You can't," I say. "Besides, I'm pretty sure people can tell the difference." I gesture toward her hideously shaped fake turkey.

"Fine," she says, snatching the label away. "But I'm not eating anything. The presence of death has ruined everything."

"You have to," I say. "It's Thanksgiving."

"It's disgusting. I don't even want to be in the same room."

"Emma, get it together," I whisper. "Don't ruin the day for Mom and Dad."

"Whatever," she says, and stomps back into the kitchen.

My mom catches my eye from the other room and gives me a worried look. I try to nod at her reassuringly, but it feels like a giant lie.

* * *

After everyone's had a drink and settled in, my dad ushers us all into our tiny dining room, and we get in line to start loading up at the buffet. Emma is in front of me. She puts tiny amounts of each of her dishes in neat little piles on her plate.

"Emma, you can take more than that. There's plenty to go around," my mom tells her.

Emma ignores her.

I fill most of my plate with mashed potatoes and a big scoop of real butter to make a butter pond. Emma gives me a dirty look because I didn't choose her gross fake kind. Nothing died to make it, so I refuse to feel guilty. Especially on Thanksgiving, when you're supposed to eat this stuff.

"Noah, you need to eat more than potatoes," my mom says.

"Way to hog it all," Emma adds.

"There's only one person behind me!"

"Whatever."

"Take some of mine if you want it. It's not like you'll eat it, anyway," I say.

The last part slips out. My mom gives me the evil eye.

"Not now that you put butter on it," Emma says. "Way to ruin everything."

"Sorry," I mutter. I take a tiny serving of her gross fake turkey to show her I mostly mean it.

My dad leans over and tells me not to make it any more of an issue. My mom gives me another warning look, as if *I'm* the one who needs a warning.

Emma whispers something to Sara, whose plate is even emptier than Emma's. I make a point not to sit near them.

When we're finally all squeezed around the dining-room table, my dad asks us to join hands to give thanks. My family says grace about three times a year: Christmas, Thanksgiving, and Easter. We're not the most religious people in the world, but my parents seem to like giving thanks for being together every so often. I always feel awkward having to hold someone's hand, but Mrs. Lamper isn't shy at all and reaches for mine. So I've got Mrs. Lamper on one side and my dad on the other, and their hand-holding styles couldn't be more different.

My dad's hands are kind of big and puffy and hot, which is gross. Also, he's squeezing the life out of my left hand. Mrs. Lamper's hands are small and fragile and cold and barely holding on. I think my hand must feel to her like my dad's feels to me, except for the hot part, I hope.

My dad clears his throat. "Thank you for the food we are about to receive. We're blessed today to be here with friends old and new, and family, and we are thinking of the loved ones we miss."

This is kind of lame as far as giving thanks goes, but it seems to please everyone.

Before we let go of hands, though, Emma pipes up.

"Let's go around the table and say what we're thankful for," she says, all fakey cheerful.

Ugh.

"Can we let go of hands?" I ask. I don't mean to be rude, but I can only be this uncomfortable for so long. Plus my dad's holding on so tight, he's cutting off the circulation to my fingers.

"No. Don't break the circle," Emma says.

My dad and Mrs. Lamper squeeze harder.

Emma motions for Sara to go first. "I'm grateful that you invited us here," Sara says. "It would have been totally boring to stay at home. No offense, Mom and Dad."

"I'm grateful to those of you who chose to eat

vegan today," Emma says. "And I'm sorry for the lives that were lost to create the rest of this meal."

"Emma!" my dad says.

"Emma's a real animal lover," my mom apologizes. She shoots Emma her warning look.

"Mitch and I are really happy to be here," Mark says quickly. "Thanks for being so welcoming."

Slowly we move around the table, and people list all the predictable things they're grateful for. Good health. Good friends. Family. Even though I have plenty of time to think of something, I still don't have a clue what to say when it's nearly my turn.

"I'm thankful for people like Jeff and Louise, who always make sure their friends have a place to go on Thanksgiving so they're not alone," Mrs. Lamper says. Her voice quivers as she says "alone," and she squeezes my hand harder. Her eyes start to brim up, but she won't let go of hands to wipe them, so her tears keep collecting, and she blinks and blinks and looks so awkward that I want to wipe them for her, but I can't because my own hands are trapped. Finally, a single drop oozes out the corner of her eye and starts to slip down her cheek. She turns to me and smiles as the drop slips down the side of her face. It is the worst combination of sad and awkward I've ever seen.

"Noah?" my dad says. "It's your turn. What are you thankful for this year?"

Who's to say? I want to ask. But don't.

I look away from the tear streak before it drops onto Mrs. Lamper's blouse. I glance around the table at all the waiting faces.

"I'm thankful for . . . um . . ."

"Say anything," Emma says impatiently.

"Anything," I say. It's our old joke.

She rolls her eyes.

"Noah, act serious," my dad says.

"I'm grateful for Thanksgiving," I say lamely.

My mom makes a disappointed face.

"I'm thankful for mashed potatoes and my family and being able to cook with my beautiful daughter," my dad says. "She's turning into an amazing cook."

I look at the seitan lump on my plate. Yeah. Amazing.

My dad was last, so we can finally let go of hands. Mine is a little wet with my dad's sweat, which is totally disgusting. I wipe it on my napkin.

Everyone starts eating, and for a little while it's quiet, except for when people say how good the food is. I guess most of it is OK. The Captain wanders in and squeezes between my and my dad's chairs to find his usual spot under the table.

I push the devil turkey across my plate and eat the stuffing and potatoes. Across the table, Emma looks very busy with her fork and knife, but neither leaves the four-inch zone above her plate.

I catch my mom noticing the same thing. Emma sees, too, and then makes a big show of putting a small piece of potato in her mouth. It looks like it causes her physical pain. I stop watching and stuff my face.

"Slow down, Noah. Jeez," my dad jokes.

"This really does taste just like turkey, Emma," Mrs. Lamper tells her, holding a wrinkled piece of fake meat on her fork. "I'll have to get the recipe from you."

"Thanks," Emma says, moving her already-moved food again.

My dad gets up for seconds and encourages everyone to follow him.

My mom keeps looking at Emma's plate and making a concerned face until Emma forces another bite down. Then another. While they do their stare-off, I sneak pieces of devil meat under the table and feed it to the dog, who licks my hand appreciatively. I feel like a rotten friend. Especially when, toward the end of dinner, there's a strange sound that starts coming from under the table. It sounds like an old man groaning.

My dad gives me a look. "Did you feed him something?"

I don't answer. Everyone stops eating to listen, which is probably a horrible idea.

A quiet whistle sound comes from under the table, and starts to get louder and more high-pitched.

"What is that?" Sara's mom asks.

My guess is they don't have a dog.

The whistle gets louder, then goes silent.

I know we have about three seconds before the actual bomb hits.

"Oh!" Emma says, covering her face.

"That damn dog," my mom says.

"Get him out of here, Noah!" my dad yells.

I push back my chair, and the Captain bolts out, knowing full well how ashamed he should be.

"Seitan farts," I say. "They are the worst."

"God, Noah!" Emma says.

"Where did your manners go?" my mom says.

My dad starts to laugh, but quickly closes his mouth because he probably doesn't want to let the smell in. Either that or make my mom mad.

People breathe into their napkins until it finally goes away, but my guess is, no one will be ready for dessert for a while.

"I guess we should clear the table," I say, which also doesn't get any laughs.

Sara, Emma, and I gather up everyone's plates while my dad brings up football to try to change the subject. Only he doesn't even know which teams are playing today.

"For someone who insisted on being in charge of almost everything we had to eat, you didn't eat much," I tell Emma while we scrape plates in the kitchen.

"Cooks never pig out on their own food," she says matter-of-factly. "They prefer to watch others enjoy it."

I wonder who she thinks enjoyed it.

She turns the hot water on and starts rinsing dishes, which she hands me to put in the dishwasher.

"It's not just today," I say. "What's going on?"

She hands me a plate that still has water on it, and it splashes over my front.

"Hey! Watch it!" I say.

"Why are you paying so much attention to what I eat?"

"Because you've been acting weird," I say. *Again,* I don't say.

I glance over at Sara, who's busy putting leftovers into plastic containers.

"And I'm your brother," I say quietly.

Instead of smiling or punching me in her affectionate way, she turns and goes back to rinsing dishes. "Stop watching every little thing I do. It's creepy."

I hate it when she gets like this. "Forget it," I say, rubbing my shirt with a dish towel. "Sorry for caring."

"We're all going for a walk!" my mom calls out from the dining room. "An old-fashioned constitutional before dessert."

"I love a Thanksgiving walk around the neighborhood," my dad says, coming into the kitchen with more dishes.

"I have to go to the bathroom first," Emma says. "Be right back."

We get our coats on and wait for what seems like forever for Emma to come back down. While she's gone, my mom gets more and more anxious and keeps whispering stuff to my dad, who pats her arm reassuringly like she's a child.

"It's just the neighborhood—you didn't have to primp," my dad tries to joke when Emma finally returns.

My mom goes over to Emma and says something, but I can't hear what it is. Whatever she says, Emma doesn't like it, because she hooks her mittened hand around Sara's arm and guides her far ahead of the group. My mom turns and gives the rest of us a forced smile.

"I love a Thanksgiving walk through the neighborhood," my dad says again, as if he hasn't already shared. He puts his arm around my mom and squeezes her close. We all follow them down the driveway. I click the Captain's leash on, and he pulls me along.

"Keep him downwind of us, Noah!" my dad says. He starts to hum a Christmas carol, and a few people join in. Some of our neighbors have Christmas lights up already, and it feels festive as we wander down the street, smelling the winter's-coming air.

Way up the road, Emma and Sara walk like a couple, heads together.

Mrs. Lamper sidles up beside me and shows me a picture Ryan texted her of him eating a giant drumstick.

"Maybe he'll bring you some leftovers," I say.

"Maybe," she says sadly.

I'm shocked to find myself hooking my own mittened hand around her arm. "It'll be OK," I tell her.

But as I feel her sadness like a shadow next to me and look up ahead at Emma hurrying away from all of us, I'm not so sure I believe it.

11

Please Stop Giving False Impressions

"You have to see Lily Smith today," Ryan tells me before I even open my locker. His breath smells like Oreos.

"It's seven fifty-five, and you're already eating cookies?" I ask. "And welcome back, by the way. How was Thanksgiving?"

"You have to *see*," he says, instead of answering.

I swivel my head around to find her.

"No!" He grabs my arm and swings me back around to face him. "Don't look!"

"You just told me to."

"I mean look, but don't *look*. Jeez. Don't be *obvious*. Here she comes. Pretend to drop something and then look up."

I drop my backpack on Ryan's foot.

"Ow!"

Lily pauses as she reaches us, just as I'm bending down to pick up my backpack.

"Hey, Noah," she says.

"Hey," I say. But I don't say it to her face, because when I look up to where her head should be, her chest is sticking out so far that it's blocking the view. I quickly look back down to hide what I'm sure is a stunned expression and hope my eyes weren't bulging out of their sockets.

Ryan nudges me to get up.

"Uh, how's it going?" I ask lamely.

"Great!" she says, smiling in a kind of flirty way. She turns and walks down the hall confidently.

"Whoa," I say when she's out of earshot.

"What do you think she has in there?" Ryan asks.

"Huh?"

"Come *on*!" he says. "Sure, people have growth spurts, but no one has a concentrated growth spurt *there*. Not that fast, anyway. Unless she ate some magic turkey for Thanksgiving."

"Maybe she has a push-up bra," I say.

"What's that?"

I don't actually know. I just overheard one of Emma's friends tell her she should get one and Emma giving her a lecture about how breast size is unimportant and beauty is on the inside. Which is pretty ironic for Emma, given her own issues with body image. What is it with people being so obsessed with their bodies? Never mind. I don't want to go there.

"I'm assuming it's something that makes your boobs look bigger," I say.

"Brilliant," Ryan says dreamily.

We finish getting our stuff and go to our first class, which is French.

"Bonjour, classe!" Madame Estelle says as we wander in. *"À vos places, s'il vous plaît."*

Once we're all sitting, Madame motions for us to open our books. *"Ouvrez vos livres à leçon quatre, s'il vous plaît."*

"Is *'quatre'* four?" Ryan whispers.

"Oui," I say. If he passes French, it will be a miracle.

I open my book to lesson four. This section is about adjectives, which we've already studied.

"Noah?" Madame Estelle asks. "*Nommez quelque chose de petite.*"

I look around the room for something small. I'm pretty sure we used Curly the last time. "*Une souris est petite,*" I say.

"What's a *souris?*" someone asks.

"*En français!*" Madame says.

"It means mouse," Molly whispers.

Madame rolls her eyes and says, "*En français!*" again. "*Ryan, nommez quelque chose de grande.*"

Ryan looks panicked. He always looks panicked when he gets called on.

"Um . . ." he says, looking around the room for something large. His eyes stop at Lily's chest.

I nudge him.

He covers his mouth to keep from laughing.

Madame comes closer. "Ryan?"

I cover my own mouth, but my body is shaking, I'm laughing so hard.

"*Noah, qu'est-ce que vous trouvez si amusant?*"

"*Rien, Madame,*" I answer.

Ryan's body is shaking now, too.

"Quittez la classe jusqu'à ce que vous pouvez vous contrôler," Madame says.

I have no idea what that means.

"Je m'excuse," Ryan says, because he probably doesn't, either.

"Maintenant," Madame says angrily.

She glares at Ryan and me until the glare scares the laughs out of us. Finally, she asks Harper something about music. I think.

I spend the rest of class trying not to make eye contact with Ryan or any part of Lily.

At lunch we go to the Community Room to eat and play foosball. We all jut our heads in Lily's direction when she's not looking. Zach cups his hands in front of his chest and mouths, "Whoa!"

"You guys are pathetic," Belle tells us.

I chew on my granola bar and keep sneaking glances at Lily's chest anyway. How *did* they get so big so fast? And doesn't she feel at all self-conscious? I know I would. Why would a girl *want* to have people staring at her chest all the time? I think about Emma again and what happened, and how what she did was kind of the opposite. Was she trying to disappear?

Curly walks over and rubs against my leg. Today she's wearing a puffy down vest. It's purple. Sadie stole it from her little sister's Teen-Me doll. I only know this because all the girls screeched, "Candy's coat!" when Curly first strutted down the hall in it, and all the boys were like, "Who's Candy?" so then we got a lesson on Teen-Me dolls, which are meant to look as realistic as possible and wear trendy clothes that cost about as much as real teen ones. I know this makes me sound sexist, but really all the girls knew, and none of the boys did—or at least admitted to.

"Currrrrlllleeeeee!" Lily runs over and picks Curly up. We all stare where we shouldn't. Even Curly looks uncomfortable, but she purrs anyway. She sounds like a squeaky motor.

"Do you have Candy's coat on today?" Lily asks in a baby voice.

Curly sniffs Lily's face.

"What are you all looking at?" Lily asks, as if she doesn't know.

We all stop looking and stare at the table instead.

"Aren't you allergic?" Sam asks.

Lily shrugs. "She just makes me a little sneezy— that's all. Right, Curly?"

Curly doesn't answer.

Lily carries Curly to the side of the table so they can watch our foosball game. I drop the little ball into the kickoff slot, and Ryan, Belle, Sam, and I grab the handles and start making our men kick their stuck-together feet at the ball. As the ball zips around the table, Curly's head darts back and forth, watching excitedly. Then, just as the ball rolls over to one of my guys, Curly leaps out of Lily's arms to make a grab for it. Only the claws on one of her back paws get stuck in Lily's shirt, and instead of landing on the table, Curly kind of bounces back to Lily's chest like a yo-yo. She dangles and squirms like a rabid animal while Lily tries to get ahold of her to untangle her claws, but all the time the front of Lily's shirt is being pulled away from her chest and showing more and more skin.

We all stand at the ends of the table, staring open-mouthed as Lily struggles with Curly's paw. None of us seems to be able to *move*. Even Belle. Finally, Lily breaks our trance by screaming, "Can I get some help here?"

We all scramble over and try to remove Curly from Lily's stretched-out shirt. Curly mews and Lily keeps screaming, "Someone get her off me!"

Finally, Belle gets hold of Curly, who kicks her back

paws frantically like a miniature kangaroo. The more she kicks, the more stretched Lily's shirt is, until finally she completely freaks out and pulls so hard that Lily's shirt drags down below her chest and her bra kind of pops out of the top, and that's when we all see how much bra there is and how little of Lily. The pads inside are like balloons.

Lily frantically pulls at her shirt one last time and manages to get Curly's claws unhooked. Curly hops to the floor and shakes herself like a wet dog, the way she always does when she's a little embarrassed. Then she races across the room and darts under one of the couches.

Belle tries to straighten Lily's shirt for her. "Maybe we should go to the girls' room," she suggests.

Lily nods, and they hurry away.

"Wow," Sam says.

"Told you," Ryan says. "Fake."

We nod.

"I never knew there was such a thing as a balloon bra," Sam says. "How many girls wear those, do you think?"

"What if they're *all* fake?" Ryan asks. "All those fantasies. Meaningless."

"Yeah, well, that's why they're called fantasies in the first place," I say.

"It's like we have to start all over again," Ryan says. "My whole list could be a sham."

I'm afraid to ask, but I do anyway. "What list?"

"Of who has the best ones."

"You have a list?" Sometimes my friends can still shock me. And what is it with people making really inappropriate lists, anyway? First Emma, and now my best friend.

"Well, just in my head. But still. It may need some major editing."

"Who's on it?" Sam asks.

Ryan looks at me guiltily.

"Emma better not be!" I say.

"C'mon, Noah, you know she's hot. Before she started wearing those baggy sweaters, anyway." He gets a dreamy look on his face.

"Whatever you're imagining right now, you need to stop," I tell him.

"Oh, relax. It's not like she'd give me the time of day. The only reason she even knows I exist is because I'm your best friend."

We throw our snack wrappers away and go to our

next class. As we pass the yellow couch, Curly pokes her head out and meows.

"Later, Curly," Ryan says. "Thanks for stealing my innocence."

She ducks back under the couch.

Our next class is science, which is my worst subject. We don't have desks, but sit at a series of tables in the shape of a horseshoe. Our science teacher, Mrs. Phelps, likes to pace inside the horseshoe and then pounce on people unexpectedly by putting her hands on the table in front of them and leaning over to get in their faces.

"Noah," she'll say, her stale coffee breath blasting in my face, "why is the oxygen atom attracted to the hydrogen atom?"

And I'll be so flustered by both her head two inches from my face and trying not to flinch from the vile smell coming out of her mouth that even if I know the answer, I can't speak.

I'm really not as dumb and useless as she seems to think I am. But I don't perform well when I'm stressed-out—and Mrs. Phelps really stresses me out. Sam says I have a sensitivity to smells and that she doesn't really have bad breath at all. But Sam can't smell his own feet, which I can smell before he even enters a room sometimes, so either he has killed all of his smell sensors with his own stench, or he is right and I have an odd and unfortunately sensitive stench sensor.

I'm pretty sure I'm not *that* sensitive, because Ryan says he sort of smells the breath, too, and definitely Sam's feet. But Ryan wears this horrible cologne that he thinks cool guys who live in "the real world" wear, so I'm pretty sure he has killed all of his own smell sensors, too.

Maybe I need to buy some cologne to mask everyone else's stench. I don't know. But whenever I get a cold and can't smell and have to breathe through my mouth, it's actually kind of a nice vacation. It's like a smell-cation.

When we get to the room, there's a girl huddle at the end of one table. Miranda, Molly, and Lily are having a summit meeting and talking way too loudly to keep it secret.

Ryan and Sam nudge me, and we go to the table at the opposite side of the room.

"No one saw," Miranda says reassuringly. "I'm telling you, Lil. Don't worry!"

"Zach saw!" Lily cries. "Did you hear what he said?"

"Don't listen to him. His mouth ruins everything," Miranda says.

Mrs. Phelps walks into class, and the girls break up.

Sam elbows me. "Should we tell her we didn't see anything?"

"If we say that, she'll know we did."

He thinks about this.

"But if we don't say anything, then she'll definitely know we know," Ryan says.

Sam looks like he's in pain, trying to figure out what to do.

"Maybe we should pretend nothing happened. Or focus on some other part of the incident. Like ask if Curly scratched her."

"You can't bring up Curly. What if a teacher finds out? They'll expel her. You know she's on probation."

"Curly's on probation?" I ask. "Since when?"

"Lily's parents figured out she's allergic and told the Tank if her symptoms get worse, they'll have to get rid of the cat."

"She should really stop picking her up. She's putting everything in jeopardy," Sam says.

This makes me feel a little less sorry for Lily, putting Curly at risk like that.

Mrs. Phelps walks into the horseshoe and clears her throat before we can figure out what to do.

"Good afternoon, friends," she says. "Who did their homework?"

We all move out of our clusters and push our chairs back to the horseshoe table.

"Noah," Mrs. Phelps says, walking over to me, "why don't you tell me what you wrote for question one?"

I quickly pull out my homework before she gets too close.

"The nucleus contains the cell's genetic information," I say.

"Good job." She spins on her heel and walks over to the other end of the table, where Lily is sitting. "Lily, are you all right?"

Lily looks up. When she does, there is a puffy red line running down her neck. She touches the scratch to try to cover it up.

"What happened?" Mrs. Phelps asks, moving closer to inspect.

Lily looks around desperately for help in making up an excuse.

"Nuh-nothing," she says. "I scratched myself somehow. I guess I need to file my nails."

"It looks like it hurts."

"I'm OK." But she seems like she's about to cry again.

"Go see Ms. Cliff and get some first-aid cream and a bandage, please."

She says this in a way that sounds like she doesn't want Lily to argue.

Poor Lily gets up, her arms crossed at her chest, and rushes out of the room.

I wonder where the pads went, and then immediately feel guilty.

Mrs. Phelps eyes all of us suspiciously before going on with class. Curly is definitely walking on thin ice.

12

Secret Santa Presents Should Come from the Heart, Not the Fruit Bowl

The week before our winter break, everyone is in a festive mood. Ms. Cliff passes around Secret Santa forms during Community Meeting and tells us to fill them out. They're to give whoever draws our name some ideas about what to get us. "And don't be silly about it," she says, all serious. "Thoughtful gifts do not need to cost money. They come from the heart."

Sam raises his hand and asks for suggestions.

"Chocolate, homemade cookies, stickers, colorful pens, erasers, mittens, hats, or artwork make good gifts," Ms. Cliff says. "World peace, money, weapons,

alcohol or other drugs, any requests for physical inter-
action (a quick hug is OK) do not."

After her lecture about how we should leave a little
gift every day leading up to our holiday celebration,
Ms. Cliff gives us a few minutes to fill out our sheets.

My sheet looks like this:

> *Name:* Noah
> *Things I like:* Candy
> *Thinks I don't like:* Vegetables

"Helpful," Ryan says when he looks at my paper.
I ignore him.

Ms. Cliff collects all our forms, mixes them up in a
bowl, and has us each draw one out.

Mine looks like this:

> *Name:* Sadie Darrow
> *Things I like:* Bubble-gum-flavored lip gloss,
>   salt-and-vinegar potato chips, bright-
>   colored socks
> *Things I don't like:* Candy

Sadie and I have a total of zero things in common.

* * *

"Who'd you get?" Ryan asks me and Sam after school. We're sitting on the bottom step outside, waiting for our rides. It's freezing out, and we're all kind of shivering as we wait.

"We're not supposed to tell," Sam says.

"You can tell *me*," Ryan says.

"I can, but I'm not going to."

"Why? Did you get me?"

"I can't believe it." Sam stands up, disgusted.

"You got me? Really?"

Sam shakes his head and walks up the steps. "I'm waiting inside."

"Nice work," I tell Ryan.

"How was I supposed to know?"

I don't have an answer.

"So, who'd you get?" he asks me.

"Have you learned nothing?"

"What?" He really doesn't see the point.

"Sadie," I say.

"You're so lucky. Figures you'd get a girl who already likes you."

"Right."

"You know I am," he says bitterly.

"Who'd *you* get?" I ask, ignoring him.

"Max. Can you believe it?" He hands me Max's description.

> *Name:* Max Fitzsimmons
>
> *Things I like:* Firecrackers, beef jerky,
> nunchucks
>
> *Things I don't like:* Secret Santas

"Everyone's a comedian," I say.

I hand him Sadie's form.

He reads her list carefully, as if he wants to memorize it. "You have it so easy! You're so lucky. I think I hate you."

"Easy? I don't know how to buy lip gloss!"

"And firecrackers are an easy purchase?"

"Just draw him pictures of everything on his list and throw in some gum," I suggest.

"Noah, you're a genius."

I nod proudly.

Mr. Lewis pulls up to get me and Harper. Emma is already in the front seat, Stu in the back. For some reason, whenever Mr. Lewis drives, he always goes to the high school first, unlike my mom, who takes turns. This means I will be squished in the back between Harper and Stu.

"Window!" I yell, even though I know it's hopeless. Harper has already jumped down the steps and is running toward the car.

Ryan smiles as he stares at Emma through the passenger window. "Can I come over? Please?"

"What are you gonna do, ride on the roof?" I ask. "There's no room."

"I could share the front seat with Emma."

"Don't make me hurt you."

"Wouldn't you prefer to have her go out with someone nice like me instead of some high-school jerk who doesn't appreciate the real Emma?"

"Do you even know the real Emma?"

He doesn't answer, and I realize I just made him feel really uncomfortable. Good.

"See you tomorrow," I say, disgusted.

"See you."

"Who'd you get for Secret Santa?" Harper asks me as soon as we pull out of the parking lot.

"I'm not telling," I say.

Emma turns to face us and reaches back to give me a punch. "I can't believe they still do that. What about the kids who don't celebrate Christmas?"

"It's Santa. It's not religious," Stu says.

"He's *Saint* Nicholas," Emma points out.

"But that doesn't have to do with Christ or anything. Does it?"

"Who cares?" Harper says. "It's just for fun."

Emma turns back to face front. "Some people are so insensitive," she says to the windshield.

When we get home, she heads straight upstairs and closes her bedroom door. Her music thrums through the walls that separate our bedrooms. I turn up my own music to drown hers out. The next thing I know, she's pounding on my door, then swinging it open without even waiting for me to tell her it's OK to come in.

The Captain gets up and rushes over to her excitedly, but she ignores him and stomps over to my bureau and turns off my music.

"What?" I ask.

"It's too loud," she says.

"Maybe yours is too loud."

"At least mine is *good*."

"What's your problem?" I ask. "Ever since Thanksgiving, you've been all moody."

She holds up her fist at me like she's threatening to hit me. She has such dry skin that her knuckles are scabby and gross-looking.

"I thought you were a pacifist," I say. "And also, ever heard of lotion? Your hands are gross."

She quickly pulls the sleeves of her sweater over her hands. "Shut up."

"Emma," I say, feeling a horrible panic in my stomach, "why are your hands like that?"

"It's not what you think. They're just dry. God."

"Emma . . ." I say again. My insides feel like they are tightening into a fist, like they do whenever I'm really scared.

"It's dry skin!" she screams at me, and storms back out of the room.

"She's insane," I tell the Captain.

He licks my sock and rolls over so I'll rub his belly.

"You'd never know you're *her* dog," I say to him. But he just thumps his tail without a care. This is the real Emma. The problem is, I don't even know what that means.

Later, when it's time for bed, Emma stands in my

doorway to say good night, just like always. "I'm sorry for yelling at you earlier," she says.

"It's all right," I say. I can tell she really means it. She looks sad, and it makes me feel scared again.

"Are you really OK?" I ask.

She nods, but just barely.

"Emma—" I start, but she interrupts.

"Sleep tight," she says. "Don't let the bedbugs bite."

"Nighty-night, bite-bite-bite," I mumble, because our childhood saying seems kind of embarrassing now.

"Chomp!" she whispers, then disappears down the hall.

The next day, I arrive at school with an upset stomach because I somehow completely forgot about Secret Santas and I don't have anything to give Sadie. I should have asked Emma if she had any unused lip gloss I could buy off her, but given her mood, I didn't bother.

Ryan and Sam come running over to me as soon as I get inside.

"Wait until you see your locker!" Sam yells, beaming.

Ryan has a you-know-what-eating grin on his face.

"How embarrassing is it?" I ask.

"It's not!" Sam says. But nothing embarrasses Sam.

"Well?" I ask Ryan.

"It's hard to say," he tells me. "You'll have to be the judge."

"Terrific."

We walk to my locker, which has a crowd of people standing around it. They step out of the way when they see me, revealing that my entire locker door is covered in Snoopy wrapping paper and a giant red bow. I glance up and down the hall at all the other lockers to see if anyone else got a wrapped door. No one did.

"Someone must really like *you*," Lily says, all baby talk.

I roll my eyes and hope that even though my cheeks feel like they are on fire, I'm not actually blushing.

"Do you think there's a present inside?" Sam asks.

"Open it!" Harper says.

"Yeah, open it!" someone else yells. Everyone starts chanting, "Open it! Open it!"

I know they won't stop until I do, so I slowly lift the handle and swing open the door.

There's nothing inside.

"Well, that's disappointing," Ryan says.

"Still cool," Sam says. "No one else got a wrapped-up door."

I wish *his* door was the one that got wrapped.

"What did you guys get?" I ask, to change the subject.

"Bag of Hershey's Kisses," Sam says.

Ryan holds up a gift bag that looks kind of wrinkled and reused. "Homemade chocolate-chip cookies. Want one?"

I reach in for a cookie and take a bite. Stale. I glance at Sam. "Useless," I tell him.

"What?" he asks innocently.

"Never mind. Hey, help me find a gift, quick. I forgot to bring something."

"You can have my cookies," Ryan says.

"Hey!" Sam yells, all offended.

"C'mon," I tell Ryan. "Let's look in the Community Room."

"Why don't you just get something from Ms. Cliff's emergency bag?"

"Because then Sadie will know I forgot."

"How?"

"All the gifts in that bag are lame. She'll know."

We scour the Community Room for anything that

could be a present, but there's nothing. I wish I had time to make something in the art room.

"I found something!" Ryan says. He runs over to the counter where the microwave and toaster are. I follow. There's a bowl beside the microwave filled with fruit. Ryan holds up a banana that is mostly brown and gross.

"I don't think so," I say.

"Hmm. How about this?" He holds up a tiny piece of fruit that looks like an orange.

"What is that?" I ask.

"It's a clementine! They're really good. Here." He hands it over.

It's kind of squishy, like it's been sitting there for a while.

"It seems kinda old. What if it's rotten inside?"

"You're making it very hard to help you," he tells me.

"Fine." I turn the clementine over in my hands. "I've got it!" I get a Sharpie out of my bag and make a face on the peel. I work really hard at it, using the grooves in the fruit to make dimples and other facial features.

"Wow," Ryan says. "You're really good! Is that . . . supposed to be Sadie?"

I make a few final touches and hold it out to him for closer inspection.

"You're a real artist, Noah! The real deal!"

I smile.

"It's so good, I bet she won't even be offended that all you got her was an inedible piece of fruit."

I ignore that. "Will you put it in her locker for me?" Ms. Cliff doesn't allow locks on lockers, because she believes in community trust or something like that.

"You got it."

He puts the fruit in his bag, and we go back to our lockers.

"Did you find something?" Sam asks when he sees us. He says it in this sort of sarcastic way, like what could we have possibly found that would be better than his stale cookies.

Ryan opens his bag and carefully shows Sam the Sadie-faced clementine so no one else can see. Then he sneaks over and puts it in her locker.

"You're giving her school fruit?" he asks. "Wow,

Noah. That is really low. Fruit is bad enough. But *school* fruit. Sheesh."

"It's art!" Ryan says.

Sam shakes his head.

"It's better than stale cookies," I say.

"They weren't stale!"

The morning bell goes off, so we head to class. I keep looking for Sadie as we walk down the hall. I wonder if she'll be able to tell I made a portrait of her, or if she'll just think she got a gross piece of fruit. But mostly I think about how Ryan called it art . . . and me the real deal.

In language arts, Mr. Marshall seems very excited to talk about our next book assignment, *A Separate Peace*. I'm so glad to be moving on from *Lord of the Flies*. He hands out copies to all of us and then notes our names and the number on our books on a sheet of paper. He reads the first chapter to us, and already I can tell this book is going to be about friendship gone wrong. These are the kinds of books I really don't like. I never understand why the characters make such obvious, horrible mistakes. It seems so unrealistic. Also, I never understand why characters in books are so over-the-top jealous of one another. Enough to do really awful things. I can't imagine that in real life. I can't imagine being so jealous of someone, especially a so-called friend, that I would want something bad to happen. But it seems to be a pretty common theme.

All day long I try to overhear Sadie talking about my gift, but she never seems to say a word. Maybe she hates it. Maybe she knows it was a last-minute gift. Maybe she's offended. Or maybe she just doesn't care.

"Did you hear anything?" I finally ask Ryan.

"What would I hear?"

"You know, Sadie telling someone about her present."

"No. Maybe she threw it out. Maybe it smelled. It was pretty old."

"It didn't smell," I say.

Sam comes over and asks what's up. "Oh, I saw it on the Tank's desk," he says.

"What was it on the Tank's desk for?" I ask.

He shrugs. "It looked like he got it as a gift."

"What? Do you think she regifted it?"

"That would be the lamest regift in history," Ryan says. "No offense."

"Thanks a lot. It's still better than stale cookies."

"They weren't stale!" Sam yells.

"There should be a rule about regifting," I say.

"Put it in the Complaint Box," Ryan suggests.

"It's the *Suggestion* Box," Sam corrects, pushing his glasses up his nose.

"Never mind," I say. "It doesn't matter." But for some reason, it *does* matter. But I don't want to explore why with these two. I just can't help wondering if maybe Ryan was wrong. Maybe I'm not a real artist after all.

13

Secret Santas Are Offensive

The last day of school before winter break, everyone walks around with winter break perma-grin. We bring our final Secret Santa gifts to Community Meeting, where we put them under a tiny fake tree on a table with a bunch of other December holiday decorations so it looks like we're celebrating more than just Christmas.

Curly has found a package with ribbons that she's started to play with. She's wearing a little Santa vest. It's red with white trim. Someone got her a Santa hat with a beard made just for cats, but no one could get close enough to put it on her.

"I guess we better start handing out these presents before Curly opens them all for us!" Ms. Cliff says.

All the teachers put on Santa hats and hand out the gifts.

I'm pretty sure Ms. Cliff got me, because every day I've been getting art supplies, like nice pencils and erasers and things like that. It would also explain the embarrassing Snoopy Christmas decorations on my locker door.

Once we get our presents, we all tear into them at the same time. I'm not sure if I'm more excited to see what mine is or to see how Sadie reacts when she opens the gift I made for her.

I keep glancing over, but there's so much paper flying through the air and people in the way that I can't see.

I open my own present, which doesn't say who it's from on the outside like it's supposed to. It's a really nice sketchbook with thick white paper. I flip through the pages and find a card.

For Noah, from Ryan. Merry Hanukkarismas. You know what I mean.

"You?" I say to him, completely shocked. "I thought you got Max! You had his card!"

"I found it on the floor. Tricked you pretty good, huh?"

"Thanks!" I say. "You're, like, the best Secret Santa ever!"

He smiles. "Draw me something sometime, OK?"

"Sure!"

Ryan opens his present from Sam. It's a black sock with a picture of an emu glued on it. "Wow," he says to Sam. "You really went all out."

"It's an emu/emo Christmas stocking!" Sam says excitedly. "Get it?"

"You know I don't celebrate Christmas, right?"

"Just look inside."

Ryan reaches in and pulls out a gift card to his favorite comics store. "I forgive you now," he says. "Thanks!"

"Where's Noah?" Ms. Cliff calls from the other side of the room. She's standing next to Sadie and some of her friends. She holds up my present. "Look what Noah Morin made for Sadie, everyone. Noah, this is beautiful!"

My cheeks burn.

"Thank you, Noah," Sadie calls from across the room. Then she blows me a kiss.

Ryan stiffens beside me like someone just insulted him.

"Way to go, Noah!" Sam says.

Everyone starts talking again like nothing happened.

"Overachiever," Ryan mumbles.

"What?" I say.

"Never mind." He picks up his emu/emo stocking and sulks off.

Even though I'm really embarrassed, I'm also proud that Ms. Cliff and Sadie like my present. It's a drawing of Sadie sitting in one of the beanbags, holding Curly. I remember seeing them like that one time, and it just seemed like a really nice moment for both of them.

"Hey, Noah," the Tank says when we're helping to clean up the wrapping paper and things. "That's a really beautiful portrait you made for Sadie."

"Thanks."

"I mean it. What a thoughtful gift. I had no idea you were so talented!" He pats me on the back. "Have a great break, OK? Do something fun."

"I'll try." I feel kind of weird, getting attention for a change. As people walk past, they say nice things to me about the drawing. It's like all of a sudden they see me differently. Like suddenly I'm worth paying a little more attention to. It feels weird. And maybe a little good.

Ryan spends the rest of the day ignoring me, and Sam spends it telling me I really need to get up the nerve to ask Sadie out. But just when I think maybe I should, I see her and Tate kissing under a fake sprig of mistletoe he holds above their heads.

Never mind.

It's a relief to go home.

Christmas Eve is my favorite night of the year. My parents always let Emma and me open one present. When we were little, the presents were usually some fun toy that we could secretly play with during the candlelight service at church. Nothing big, but something special. As we've gotten older, they give us sort of lame things, like pajamas with a Christmas theme. But even though they're silly, we put them on and decorate cookies and stay up late, pretending we still believe in Santa Claus. We also go to the evening service at church because my mom loves singing all the old Christmas hymns, and how they turn out the lights and sing "Silent Night" as everyone lights tiny candles they hand out at the beginning of the service.

We're all ready to go except Emma, who is taking forever in the bathroom. My parents pace the hall in their nice Christmas Eve clothes while I fidget with my tie because I hate how it feels to have my shirt buttoned up against my neck.

"Emma, for the tenth time, you need to hurry up! We're going to be late!" my mom says.

I catch my dad making a sort of cringed expression. The longer she takes, the more on edge they seem to get. This whole scene feels familiar in the worst way.

My mom reaches for my dad's hand as they stand outside the bathroom door. The Captain paces the hall nervously and whines.

But Emma doesn't come out.

We wait five more minutes. Then ten. She doesn't respond.

"Emma," my dad says. I can hear the impatience and worry battling inside his voice. "I'm going to give you one more minute, and then I'm going to bang this door down if I have to."

My mom leans against the wall and looks up at the ceiling. I wonder if I got that from her. I wonder if she's saying a prayer. I wonder if she's wishing we went to church more, to improve her chances of having her prayer come true. I know what she's praying for, so I add my own to it to improve our chances.

Please, God. Please don't let her be sick again.

My dad jiggles the door handle one more time.

My mom seems to sink into the wall.

I walk over to them and knock on the door myself.

"Emma? It's me. If they go away, will you open up?"

I motion for my mom and dad to step away. I hear the faucet turn on, then off again. The toilet flushes. Everything is in the wrong order. I press the side of my face against the door.

"Can you hear me?" I ask.

The sound of bare feet on tile comes closer to the door. The door jiggles a little, and I know she's pressing her head against it on the other side.

"Emma?"

She jiggles the doorknob in response.

"Will you come out?"

She scratches her fingers along the door, like a cat.

I turn toward my parents. *Go away,* I mouth.

They nod and go to their bedroom.

"They're gone," I say quietly. "Now, open up."

I hear a click and know she's unlocked the door. Slowly it moves inward, and I slip inside.

Her hair is wet and smells like puke, even from a few feet away.

She's wearing only a T-shirt and leggings. I feel my own stomach heave when I see her: the true shape of her that she's been hiding under her sweaters for months.

"I'm sorry," she says, looking at the floor. "I didn't want to eat so much for dinner, but I knew it would make Mom and Dad happy to see me do it. Only, I . . . it made me feel so sick. I—couldn't keep it down. I couldn't—"

"Emma," I say, "why did this happen again? Why didn't you try to stop it?" All these feelings I've been trying to hold back start to rise in my stomach, then my chest. All the worry I kept buried there is like a tidal wave rising inside me, waiting to explode out of my mouth, but I don't know if it will be in the form of crying or yelling. How could she do this again? Why?

She sits on the edge of the tub and hides her face in her hands. "I don't want to be like this! I can't help it!"

Her knuckles are raw. I bite my lips shut to keep the wave of rage and fear inside my mouth. *Why* can't she help it?

"I'm sorry," she says again.

Her body starts to shake. I go over to her and put my arm around her.

"No," I say. It's all I can let escape me. *No. Not this again.*

She leans her head into me and tries to hug me, but she slips onto the cold floor.

"Mom!" I yell. It's just one word, but it's so loud and has so much fear in it that my parents come running, horror on their faces before they even see Emma on the floor.

There are lots of "oh, Emma's" and "oh, baby's" and other things I can't hear. Can't listen to. The fear and panic from the people who are supposed to be in control is too scary. I get up to leave, but as I step into the hall, heavy footsteps follow. My dad is carrying Emma like she's as light as a baby in his arms.

"Noah, get some blankets and meet me at the car," my dad says.

My mom rushes past and into Emma's room in search of some clothes.

In the car, my mom sits in the backseat, cradling Emma in her arms. I sit up front with my dad. We drive through town, past our candlelit church. If I rolled down my window, I bet I could hear them singing "Silent Night." My chest feels tight and achy and almost empty now that the wave has escaped. I don't even think I knew just how much worry I was holding inside until I let it all out. But I don't feel relief. I just feel . . . a different kind of terror. All our fears came true. It didn't matter how careful we were. How hard we tried to do everything Emma wanted. How much therapy Emma went to. We couldn't stop it from coming back. My heart presses against my chest with each beat, like it does when I'm nervous. Only a million times harder.

When we get to the hospital, my parents get Emma checked in. Then my dad comes to wait with me while my mom goes with Emma, who looks like a ghost already. The waiting room is empty. There's a TV screen on the wall that's on but muted, so you can see the newscasters talking but you can't hear what they're saying. One of them is wearing a Santa hat. If Emma saw, she'd make a comment about how insensitive that is to people who don't celebrate Christmas, and then I'd make a comment about how she needs to lighten up. And then my parents would tell us to stop bickering, and everything would feel normal. But instead I just stare at the Santa hat and watch the person talk with no words coming out. And I think, *Emma was right. Santa hats are offensive.*

I feel like I'm going to throw up, but I know I can't. I fiddle with my tie, which feels like it's choking me.

My dad leans forward and grabs the sides of his head with his hands, cupping his ears as if the sound of the TV is not only on but too loud. Finally, he leans back in his chair and turns to me.

"Did you know it was this bad?" he asks. "Tell me the truth."

My heart twists in my chest. I know he wants me to say no so he can say no, too. And then he won't feel guilty for not stepping in sooner. For not saying enough is enough with all her rules about food and how increasingly nutty they were getting. Not that it would matter. You can't force someone to eat. And even if you could figure out a way, they can just puke it up.

My dad stands and walks across the room, then comes back again. Back and forth, like he's trying to walk away from the truth.

"I thought if we just did what she wanted and followed her rules, she'd eat. She'd be OK. I'd do anything as long as it meant she'd eat . . ."

He walks across the room, then comes back again.

"I thought with all the cooking and meal planning, she was in control. She even seemed happy. Didn't she seem happy to you?"

He looks at me to say yes, to agree with him, but I can't.

He sits and grabs the sides of his head again. "Oh, God," he says. A sob escapes from somewhere deep down in his chest, as if his own heart squeezed out the pain.

"Why?" he asks the empty room.

Why?

But the room doesn't have any answers.

Later, a doctor comes out to tell us what's happening. They put a tube in her arm to hydrate her. My mom refuses to leave her side. She can spend the night with her. They've admitted her to care and will transfer her to the psych department in the morning.

Merry Christmas to us.

"Would you like to discuss the details in private?" the doctor asks my dad.

"There's no one here," my dad says, looking around the empty waiting room.

The doctor motions to me.

"How bad is it?" my dad asks.

"She's severely dehydrated. And"—he pauses—"as I'm sure you know, dangerously underweight."

I detect an accusing tone, and I can tell my dad does, too. He starts to reach for his ears again, then stops.

"Why didn't her therapist tell us how serious things were getting?" my dad asks. "I thought she was doing OK. Not great, but OK. We were trying all these recipes together!"

I don't point out that trying new recipes isn't the same as eating.

"She's been making herself vomit regularly. We can discuss the damage caused to her—"

"Don't," my dad interrupts. "I—I don't think I can hear it right now. Just tell me how long it will be until she's OK. Can she come home soon?"

"It depends on how she responds to treatment."

"Well, she's not going back to her regular therapist—that's for sure," my dad says.

"We need to get her back to a stable condition," the doctor says, ignoring him. "Then we can evaluate her mental state. Right now, we don't really know what we're working with."

"You're working with my daughter!"

The doctor nods calmly. "I know that."

My dad gets up again and starts pacing. The reporters on TV are laughing. The guy with the Santa hat shakes his head so the pom-pom on top flips from side to side. The woman shoves his shoulder playfully.

My dad is crying.

The doctor looks at me and smiles like an idiot. I know he's trying to be reassuring, but he must know he can't be, so why bother?

"I'll go check on your wife and daughter now, but if you have any questions, you can call me." He hands my dad a card. "You should probably go home and get some rest."

"I want to see Emma before I go," my dad says.

The doctor nods. "I'll take you."

"Noah," my dad says, "will you be all right here?"

"Can't I go?" I ask.

"I think it would be best if you stayed here," the doctor says. "She's sleeping now, anyway."

"I'll be right back," my dad says. He follows the doctor out of the room, leaving me alone.

The newscasters are showing a fake satellite on a screen with Santa and his sleigh zooming above the planet. I glance around the empty room. I don't remember when I stopped believing in Santa Claus. It might have been the same time as when I stopped thinking there was really a God, not that my family has ever been very religious. When I was really young, I thought God and Santa were kind of the same guy. Some supernatural being that could see you and know when you were misbehaving. You were supposed to be good for Santa and good for God. One gave you presents, and one gave you heaven. To a kid, those things seemed kind of equal.

But everyone stops believing in Santa at some point. So what makes God so special? At least you could rely on Santa coming to save the day once a year. You had real evidence of his existence. But God? What did God ever do to provide any proof that being good would pay off someday? It seems I know plenty of good people who never got a thing for it. If anything, God was a much bigger disappointment than Santa ever was.

I lean my head back against the wall and close my eyes. Out in the hall, a nurse wishes another nurse "Merry Christmas" as she leaves her shift. She's wearing a bright-red coat and a green scarf.

"Hope you get caught under the mistletoe!" she calls cheerfully.

"You too!" the other one calls back.

I don't know how anyone could be cheerful in a place like this. Where my sister is lying in bed, trying to disappear.

"Noah." My dad squeezes my shoulder. I didn't even hear him come back. "It's time to go."

"What about Mom?" I ask.

"She's staying."

I follow my dad out to the parking lot. The sky is perfectly black, with the stars shining especially bright.

I bet the Christmas carolers back in our neighborhood are walking down our street right now, talking about what a perfect Christmas Eve night it is. How beautiful. How peaceful. Maybe they're joking about mistletoe, too. Maybe they're looking up in the sky for Santa's sleigh. I imagine him flying overhead, just like on TV. But instead of landing on our roof and leaving a bunch of presents, he flies right past our house without stopping. No Christmas for us this year.

Ho, ho, no.

14

Every Christmas morning, I'm the first to wake up. I lie in bed listening to the quiet, imagining the magic waiting for us downstairs. I picture the stockings stuffed to overflowing, each on a chair or the couch— our designated present-opening spot. When I can't wait another second, I get up, throw some warm socks on, and head for Emma's room.

She's always sleeping with her face to the wall, so I reach over and shake her. "It's Christmas!" I yell. "Time to get up!"

She likes to moan and groan and act like she's too tired, but she gets up pretty quickly and finds her slippers, and then the two of us go to my parents' room. My mom has to go down first to turn on the tree lights, and then she calls to tell us everything's ready and "Santa came!" and "Oh, boy, was he good to you this year!" and all that stuff. Emma and I race down the stairs side by side. Sometimes we even hold hands. My dad follows, telling us to slow down or we'll take a nosedive and ruin Christmas. Then we get to the bottom of the stairs, and the living room feels all magical, like maybe it really was Santa Claus who left all the presents, not my groggy-eyed parents at one in the morning when we finally fell asleep. We find our stockings and ooh and aah over the stuff spilling out of them, but we have to sit and settle down and then take turns pulling things out to make the morning last and last. It's the very best part of Christmas.

When I wake up, I look at the Super Ball marks on my ceiling and listen to the quiet, imagining the magic waiting downstairs. Then I remember that there probably isn't any.

The Captain thumps his tail when he realizes I'm awake. He jumps up on my bed and licks my ear. I roll over to make room for him. He stretches out along my side, pressing against me. In all his excitement at being allowed on the bed, he lets out a whistler and I have to tuck my head under the covers for a while until it passes.

"You really do know how to smell up a place," I tell him.

He thumps his heavy tail.

We wait for a while, then finally get up. The Captain follows me to Emma's room and whimpers for her. I sit on her neatly made bed. It's always neatly made, as far as I can tell. I look around, wondering when I came in here last. Maybe it was a whole year ago—since last Christmas. She's taken down some of the band posters she used to have. Now the pale-green walls are almost bare except for her favorites, neatly hanging there like an art display. On her nightstand there's an old family photo of the four of us from before we had the Captain. From before the first time she got sick. We look so young and normal.

Emma's backpack is on the floor, her books spilling out. I go over and zip them inside. I don't know why. It just seems like Emma wouldn't want her space to be untidy. I open the shades to let some sun in. The Captain follows me. I pet his head and he makes a sad noise, then licks my hand.

"What are you doing in here, Noah?"

My dad stands in the doorway, looking like he hasn't slept.

"Just letting some light in, I guess."

"That's nice."

"Have you heard from Mom yet?"

"She texted me a few times through the night. Emma's stable and sleeping."

"Is Mom OK?"

He shrugs.

"Merry Christmas," I say.

"Oh," he says. "Right. Merry Christmas, buddy." He hugs me. He smells like stale clothes and morning breath. And worry.

I squeeze my arms around him and wish I could just keep holding on, but he pulls away from me and sighs like he has never been so tired in his life.

"Are we going back to the hospital?" I ask.

He nods. "Go take a shower and I'll make some breakfast."

"OK." I walk out to the hallway and wait for him

to follow, but he doesn't. Neither does the Captain. I listen, wondering what he's doing in there. But then I hear him crying, and I wish I had just gone to the stupid shower.

There's almost no traffic on the road on our way to the hospital. We drive past houses decorated with colored lights, and I imagine the people inside, all cozy and happy and opening presents. My phone buzzes in my pocket, but I don't look to see who it is. Sam or Ryan, most likely. I wonder if they heard about what happened yet. I wonder if anyone has, or if they're all just assuming I'm home opening presents like everyone else who celebrates Christmas.

"You might have to stay in the waiting room for a while," my dad says. "Did you remember to bring something to read?"

"No."

"Oh, Noah. You'll just have to look at magazines, then."

"Whatever."

We get out of the car and go to the reception area to find out where Emma is, then follow signs through the maze of halls until we find the room.

"Let me check with Mom before we go in," my dad says.

"I'm not five," I tell him. "I can handle it."

"Just let me check."

He leaves me standing in the hall. The nurses are all wearing Santa hats. One of them starts coming toward me with a mini candy cane. It is the absolute last thing I want right now, so I open the door to my sister's room and duck inside.

"Noah, I told you to wait!" my dad hisses.

Emma is curled up with her back to me, just like she is every Christmas morning. But this time, there's a tube attached to her somewhere, and my parents are standing beside her bed, holding each other up. They pull apart as soon as my mom sees me. She wipes her eyes.

"You shouldn't be in here, Noah," she says.

"Where should I be?" I ask.

And Merry Christmas to you, too, I don't say out loud.

"We should talk in the hall," my dad says.

My mom reaches out and touches Emma's back before we go, so I do, too. She doesn't move. She's covered in blankets, so I don't know if she can feel my hand or not. I wonder if she's just pretending to be asleep. Just in case, I press a little harder, so she knows it's me.

"Don't wake her," my mom whispers.

"I wasn't. I was just—"

Trying to be sure of her.

In the hall, my mom explains that the doctor wants to send Emma to a treatment center, just like last time. But a different one, that's had better results. "There's more staff there," she says. "He thinks she'll get better therapy, too."

"Where is it?" my dad asks.

"Outside of Boston."

"But that's over two hours away!"

"Keep your voice down. I know. But isn't it worth it? If they can help her for good this time?"

My dad leans against the wall. "But it's so far. What if something happens? We won't be able to see her every day."

"They don't want us to. They think she needs . . . to be away from us."

"How the hell is that supposed to help?"

"Keep your voice down."

One of the Santa nurses starts walking toward

us, and my mom gives my dad a look like, *Nice going.*

"Merry Christmas!" the nurse sings. There's a bell on the pom-pom of her hat.

I feel like telling her we don't celebrate. This year, it wouldn't even be a lie.

My mom smiles at her, but my dad turns away.

"Would you like some hot chocolate?" the nurse asks me.

"No, thanks."

"Have some, Noah," my mom says. "Did you eat breakfast?"

"Yes," I say. "I'm the one you don't have to worry about, remember?"

She frowns at me, and I feel terrible. I don't even know why I said it. The nurse gives us a strange look and walks away.

"That was rude," my mom says.

"Sorry."

"Let's go to the cafeteria. I need some coffee." She leads the way.

Even though I tell her I don't want anything, she gets me a hot chocolate. We sit at the only crumb-free table next to a window. Spits of snow are falling down, and the cars in the parking lot have a thin layer of white on them. They look like ghosts.

We sit at the table, sipping our drinks and not talking.

My dad keeps sighing and looking out the window. My mom clutches her paper coffee cup in both hands, staring at the plastic lid as if somewhere inside the tiny hole in the top are all the answers of what to do next.

A doctor walks over to us. "Mr. and Mrs. Morin?"

My parents nod.

"One of the nurses said she thought she saw you come this way. I'm Dr. Sawyer, from New Horizons. Can we talk?"

"Noah, do you remember how to get to the waiting room?" my dad asks.

"Yeah," I say. I get up and leave them and wander down the hall.

Instead of going to the waiting room, though, I find Emma's room and stand outside. No one seems to notice me or care that I'm here, so I open the door and go in.

Emma is still curled up in her bed facing the wall. I go over and sit in the chair next to her. The plastic creaks when I sit down, and she stirs a little but doesn't seem to wake up. I follow the clear tube coming from a plastic bag attached to a tall metal holder next to the bed. It's attached somewhere to her body under the covers. Drips fall from the bag every second or two, silently hydrating my sister.

"Merry Christmas," I whisper quietly.

"Merry Christmas," she whispers back.

I jump up and lean over her to see her face. Her eyes are closed.

"Emma?"

"I'm here."

She turns her head just barely, but enough to face me. Her lips are so chapped, there's dried-up blood in the creases. She opens her eyes just a slit. It's good to see her, even like this. Just to see that her eyes can still open.

"Hey," I say.

"Hey. Sorry I ruined Christmas." Her voice is raspy and hard to hear.

"Are you OK?"

She closes her eyes and doesn't answer.

I reach out and touch her shoulder through the blankets. It's like grabbing a chicken bone.

"Why, Emma?" I ask. "Why did you do it again?"

Tears form in her closed eyes. They slowly gather in the corners and slip down her temples.

"I don't understand," I say. "I don't know how you can make yourself so sick."

"Neither do I," she says through her broken lips.

Her hand moves from under the blanket, so I pull the cloth back to find it. It's the arm with things attached, and I want to cover it back up to hide the needle sticking into the top of her hand, but she wiggles her fingers, so I hold her hand and she squeezes mine back.

Finally, she opens her eyes to look at me. "I'm sorry," she says again, then lets go.

"I don't know what to say," I tell her.

"I know."

"What can I do?"

"Don't hate me."

I want to say I won't, but I can't force the words out.

"I'm so tired," she says. "Will you stay with me if I go to sleep?"

"Sure."

I sit back down and listen to her breathing until it steadies out and I can tell she's really sleeping again. I lean my head against the side of the railing and close my eyes.

Get better, I say in my head. *Please let her get better right now,* I pray to God and Santa and anyone else who might have some magical power.

But I know she can't just magically be cured. She'll have to go to a treatment center before she can come home again. And when she comes back, she'll be different. Just like last time. She will be some new version of Emma that she thinks will make life easier. And maybe it will, and maybe it won't. Maybe it will last, and maybe it won't. But we'll all walk around pretending either way, secretly terrified of this thing inside her that no one seems to understand or be able to stop. Why does she have to be the bird that can't change?

Why can't she see she's starving not just herself but also everyone who cares about her?

I move my hand across the covers until I can feel her back somewhere under there. I press so I can feel her breath go up and down.

Why do you do this? I ask her in my head.

I feel her back rise just slightly, letting me know she's still here, but that's all. No answers, as usual. There's no explanation that makes any sense, anyway.

Later, when my parents come back, my dad tells me he's taking me home again. I stand up and stretch and wait for my mom to at least hug me good-bye, but she kind of collapses into the chair and rests her head on the railing, just where mine was.

"C'mon," my dad says. He reaches for Emma's side and places his hand where her hip might be, then squeezes his eyes shut, as if he's making a wish. I reach out and touch her, too, and make the same wish I made earlier. *Get better. Get better right now.*

But of course it doesn't come true. There is no Santa. And I bet there's no God, either.

15

Welcome-Back Hugs Should Be Limited to Five Seconds

I climb out of my dad's car and stand in the parking lot facing the school. Harper jogs ahead happily, and my dad leaves with Stu for the high school. Even after the car pulls away, I just stand there. I watch other people get out of their cars and hug as they go inside together. Everyone seems so happy to be back. They probably all had great vacations. They probably slept late and texted one another all day saying how great it is to not have to do *anything*. They probably met up in town to see a movie or whatever. They probably had sleepovers and gossiped about who would still be dating when we got back to school. They probably asked one another, "Did you hear what happened to Noah's sister?"

My phone battery died on Christmas Day, and I never bothered to charge it.

"Noah!" It's Ryan. He slams the door of his mom's car. She waves and smiles at me sadly. I don't know if her sadness is for me or her own loneliness, and it just makes me feel worse.

"Hey!" He runs over and half hugs me like all the guys do. "You didn't return any of my calls," he says.

I don't know how to answer.

"Sorry to hear about Emma."

We stand there quietly, letting the cold seep into our feet and up our legs.

The good thing about a friend like Ryan is you don't have to explain anything to him. You can just stand next to him and be miserable and somehow he knows all you need is a friend to stand next to and not ask you any questions.

The door of the school opens, and Sam comes bounding down the steps without a coat on. He trudges across the slushy parking lot in a determined way.

"What are you guys doing out here?" he asks cheerfully.

"Contemplating the mystery of such a poorly plowed parking lot," Ryan says.

"Ms. Leonard has poor eyesight," Sam says. "It's not her fault. Plus the plow doesn't even fit on her truck right. Her son cobbled it together for her."

Sam turns to me. "Hey, Noah. It's good to see you. Vacation wasn't the same without you."

Normally during vacation, the three of us hang out practically every day, taking turns staying at each other's house. But this year I guess they did all that without me. What did I do? Sat in my room mostly, and listened to my parents arguing about how Emma could get so sick so fast. About how on earth they're going to pay the part of Emma's treatment not covered by insurance. About how they'll have to find a new therapist when Emma comes home. About basically everything. I stayed in bed and drew, using the paper and pens Ryan gave me for Christmas. I drew and drew and tried not to listen, but I couldn't help it. Instead of drawing a picture for Ryan like I promised, I filled every page of the sketch pad before I even realized I was drawing so much. Page after page of angry colors fighting one another to fill every corner of white. The same bird flying across the page, not changing, but traveling on, leaving me and my parents alone. The beast from *Lord of the Flies* chasing it out of our reach. My parents turned into angry monsters, tearing each other apart. And then when I couldn't draw figures anymore, I filled the pages with colors that felt like fear and hate and loneliness. Pages that looked like how my insides felt. Scared. Helpless. Alone.

"So . . . how's Emma doing?" Sam asks quietly.

I breathe in the winter air and let it sting inside my chest. "OK," I say.

Sam looks like he wants to ask more, but Ryan cuts him off. "Let's go in. It's freezing out here."

We slowly walk across the parking lot, jumping over piles of dirty slush.

Inside, the school feels smaller somehow. And louder. And happier. Has everyone always been this happy?

Ms. Cliff comes toward me and asks if I'll talk to her in her office.

"I'm fine," I tell her. Ms. Cliff is notorious for making students talk about their "problems" for hours.

She puts her hand on my shoulder. "I'd still like to talk to you. Just for a minute."

I follow her down the hall. People get quiet as we

walk by and look at me with their sad "I feel so sorry for you" faces. But I know as soon as I pass, they go right back to being happy again.

Ms. Cliff closes her office door and motions for me to sit in the saggy couch against the wall. She sits across from me in a rocking chair.

She watches me for a minute, then takes a loud deep breath in and out.

"I was so sorry to hear about Emma's relapse," she says, leaning forward.

Why are you sorry? It's not your fault, I don't answer.

"I know it must be hard at home, with Emma away."

I'm sure she thinks it's hard. But I bet she doesn't really know what that means. My mom crying all the time. My dad pacing all the time. Me hiding in my room with the Captain all the time. Us sitting at the table for dinner, forcing ourselves to eat, even though swallowing hurts. And all I can think as I feel the food push down my throat is how I wish it was going down Emma's. I wish she was sitting in the empty chair across from me. I wish we had realized how serious her behavior was, that it wasn't just "Emma quirks." I wish we hadn't trusted her.

"Noah? Do you want to talk about it?"

Curly comes out from under the couch. I reach for her, and she touches my finger with her cold wet nose.

Ms. Cliff waits for me to answer.

Curly rubs her body against my leg. She's wearing a green sweater with a red heart on the back.

I pat my thighs and she jumps up, circles on her pointy feet a few times, then settles down. Her warmth presses through my jeans. I pet her over her sweater and she starts to purr.

Someone knocks on the door and opens it before waiting for Ms. Cliff to say "Come in."

The Tank peeks his head inside. "Oops. Sorry to interrupt."

Curly looks up at the sound of his voice and makes her happy chirping noise.

"Community Meeting is about to start," he says. He nods at me. "Hey, Noah. It's good to see you."

"Hey," I say quietly. I wonder if he means it. Is it *really* good to see me? Why? My being here doesn't mean I'm OK or fine or something. It just means I don't want to be home. It means I couldn't stand to be there for another second. It means there was nowhere else to go.

"Go ahead and start without us," Ms. Cliff says.

He shuts the door.

"Noah? I just want you to know that I'm here if you decide you want to talk about anything. About Emma, or about anything you want."

I pet Curly harder. She stops purring.

"We all care about Emma," Ms. Cliff says. "And I know you must be worried sick. But your mom said she's getting good care. That she's making progress."

"I guess so." I haven't seen or talked to her since we said good-bye at the hospital, just before they took her to New Horizons, also known as "Puker Prison." That's what Emma whispered in my ear when we hugged good-bye. "Come visit me at Puker Prison," she said. "Promise?"

She looked at us like we were abandoning her. Like we were sending her to some kind of jail. When we were little and we finished eating everything on our plates, my dad would say, "You belong to the Clean Plate Club!" New Horizons is like a jail for all the people who can't make it into the club.

The whole drive home from the hospital, my mom cried quietly and my dad tapped his fingers on the steering wheel uncomfortably and I sat in the backseat, staring out the window, feeling like the worst brother in the world.

"She's in a safe place," Ms. Cliff says.

"Can I go to Community Meeting now?" I ask.

She does that deep-breath thing again, then stands up.

"Sure," she says. "Let's go."

Curly jumps down and mews, then slips under the couch again.

We start to walk down the hall, but I stop. "I'm just going to get something from my locker," I say.

"All right. I'll see you there."

I wait for her to disappear down the hall, then close my locker and press my forehead against the cold metal. I don't want to go to Community Meeting. I don't want to walk in late and have everyone look at me and feel sorry for me or wonder how my family could have been so stupid not to see how sick Emma was. I don't want them to wonder how we could have let things get so bad. I'm sure that's what they're all thinking. I would.

There's a faint clicking sound as Curly walks down the hall. She stops to sniff my leg, then keeps going.

I decide to go to the art room and wait for the stupid meeting to be over and hope Ms. Cliff doesn't come find me and ask why I never showed up.

The art room smells like turpentine and paper and eraser. I find some of the projects I left to be fired over vacation. There's the bowl I made, and some things I meant to be Christmas presents but didn't finish in time. The shiny blue glaze for the bowl came out just right. Inside, there's a note from Ms. Cliff that says, "Beautiful, Noah! A+." I don't feel like giving it to my parents anymore, so I leave it on Ms. Cliff's table and write "Thank you" on the note, hoping that's enough to let her know I want her to have it.

I find the bag of clay and take a chunk out, then pour some water in a paper cup. Curly peeks her head around the corner.

"I thought you were going to Community Meeting," I say.

She slinks around the room, rubbing against the legs of the tables.

I start to shape my clay, wetting it with water from

my cup. I don't really think about what I'm making; I just start to shape it, letting my hands move over the clay and push and form it. There's a head, I think. And a body. But I try not to label the shapes as they form. I keep working, not paying attention to Curly as she hops up on the table and sniffs the clay.

I find my clay shaper and begin to make lines. A face. Hair. Arms. Legs.

And wings.

As I carve and scrape away, the figure gets smaller and smaller.

A loud noise outside startles me. Meeting is over. A herd of people pass by the partly open door. I quickly cover my figure with a damp cloth and rush to class to avoid being late and having to walk in on everyone. But I spend the whole day wanting to sneak out of class and go back to the art room. Back to my figure. Back to shaping and sculpting and not having to think about anything else. Back to just being alone.

16

If You Are Going to Share Details About Your Love Life, Please Learn the Bases

"Did you hear Curly's sick?" Sam asks when I get to school the next morning.

"What do you mean?"

"I don't know. The Tank had to take her to the vet last night."

"Maybe she got rabies from a mouse after all," Ryan says.

"That's not funny," I say.

"I wasn't trying to be funny."

The Tank walks toward us. "Noah? Can I talk to you?"

I follow the Tank to his classroom. Why do all the teachers want to talk to me? I'm not the one in the hospital.

"Were you working in the art room yesterday?" he asks once we're alone.

"Yes."

"Did you put your project away properly?"

I try to remember. "I—I think so. I put cloth over my project so it wouldn't dry out."

"Did you put it on the storage rack where Curly couldn't reach it?"

My heart sinks. I shake my head.

"Do you remember the rule about that?"

My throat feels like it has a giant piece of food stuck in it.

"We can't leave anything out that Curly might get into. Anything she might think is food."

Something shifts in my gut.

"Did—? Is she—?"

"She had to stay at the vet's overnight for observation. I'm not sure how she'll be yet." He walks over to his desk and opens a drawer. He pulls out something wrapped in the same cloth I used in the art room yesterday. Carefully, he starts to unwrap it, then holds the clay object out to me. It's my figure. But the face has been smoothed out and the details erased where Curly must have licked it.

The figure is small but powerful. It has long, strong arms and legs, and a round, full belly. And bird wings. The Tank looks more concerned about the shape of what I was making than he is about anything else.

"Did you make this?" he asks.

I blink several times, but my eyes still water.

I nod.

"It's beautiful, you know," he says. "Is it supposed to be anyone in particular?" But he knows the answer. I'm sure he does. And I feel ashamed that he saw this, because I don't know if he'll understand what I was trying to do. I don't even know if *I* understand. But I was thinking about Emma, and this is the shape that emerged. The shape I wish she could be in real life. A bird that I *could* change.

Tears slip down both sides of my face, gathering along my jaw. I quickly wipe them away.

"I don't know," I lie.

He sets the sculpture gently on his desk and wraps it up again.

"Noah, did you talk to Ms. Cliff about what happened over vacation? To Emma?"

"Not really."

"Why not?"

"I didn't know what to say."

"Do you want to talk to me instead?"

I wipe my face again. I think of Curly in some cage at the vet's. I think of Emma in some cage near Boston. Why couldn't I be more careful? Why couldn't I pay more attention?

"It's my fault," I say. "Everything's my fault."

"We all make mistakes," the Tank says. "Curly's tough. I'm sure she'll be all right in a day or so."

My nose starts to run.

"Why don't you sit down," he says.

"I ruin everything," I say, pacing instead of sitting. "I should have confronted Emma better. I should have forced her to admit what was going on. Or stopped her somehow. Told my parents. I mean, not that they didn't already know. Why are we all so useless? Why couldn't we help her?"

The door opens, and the Tank waves his hand at whoever started to come inside to go away.

He walks over to me and puts his hands on my

shoulders so we're face-to-face. "You know, Noah, you're only responsible for one person in this world."

I shake my head. "No. I could have helped her."

"I'm serious. We can work to be kind. We can work to be generous. We can be fair and responsible. But in the end, we can't prevent people—or animals—from making their own choices, and their own mistakes, like Curly, if they're determined."

"But I *could* have—I *should* have."

He squeezes my shoulders tight with his huge, strong hands. "You can't change what happened. No one could. Only Emma. She has a disease, Noah. A really complicated one. What happened isn't your fault. But it's what you do now that counts."

"But there's nothing I *can* do. That's the problem!"

"You can let Emma know that you love her. You can let her know how much she matters to you." He lets go of me and gets a tissue from his desk.

"Here," he says, handing it to me. "Do you want to go hang out in Ms. Cliff's office for a while?"

I wipe my face off with the tissue. "Not really."

"Yeah." He grins. "I don't blame you."

He takes my soggy tissue and throws it away.

"I'll let you know as soon as I hear from the vet.

OK? Curly—she'll be OK. And I bet Emma will be, too."

I nod, wanting to believe him.

He hands me the clay figure, but I push it back.

"I don't want it," I say.

"But Noah, it's really good. I mean, you're really talented. You know that, right?"

"It doesn't matter."

"Sure it does. Why would you say that?"

"There are just—more important things. Art's a waste of time."

He looks disappointed to hear me say that. "Someday you'll know that's not true."

He puts the figure back in a drawer in his desk.

"You ready to start class?"

"I guess."

I go over to my seat and he opens the door. Students file in quietly and seem to avoid looking at me. I don't know if it's because they feel sorry for me because of Emma or hate me because I might have killed Curly.

The Tank starts class, but I don't really hear what he says. I just watch him pace around in front of the room, and I tune out. I think again about Emma and Curly in their unfamiliar cages, wondering what they're thinking right now. If they're scared. If they're in pain. But mostly if they'll be OK, like the Tank said.

After class, I try to become part of the herd, moving from one subject to another. None of the teachers call on me, and no one really talks to me. At lunch, I go outside and sit on the steps, even though it's freezing out and I don't have a lunch, because I was used to that being Emma's job and forgot I had to make my own now. Ryan finds me within a few minutes. He hands me my coat. Sam follows and hands me a bag of trail mix. They sit on either side of me and eat their lunches. I eat the trail mix one piece at a time. Peanut. Raisin. M&M. Sunflower seed. The cold air swirls around us, stinging our faces. My fingers start to feel numb, but I keep eating. Peanut. Raisin. M&M. Sunflower seed.

"Molly and I got to second base during vacation," Sam says when I'm about halfway through the bag.

I stop eating.

"Wow, Sam. I'm sure Noah was dying to hear that," Ryan says.

"Well, I just thought he should know."

"Why?"

"Because we tell each other everything! Or we're supposed to."

Ryan crumples up his paper lunch bag into a ball.

"What part of second base?" I ask, just to keep Ryan from losing his temper.

"Kissing," Sam says.

"Kissing is first base," Ryan says. "And we already know you've kissed. We've seen you!"

"With tongues!" Sam says. "And I thought holding hands was first base."

"No, holding hands is like . . . stepping up to the plate. It doesn't really count as a base."

"Oh. Well, then, I got to first base," Sam says.

"And how was it?" Ryan asks sarcastically.

"Pretty amazing, actually. Even when she stuck her tongue in my mouth."

Ryan squeezes his lunch bag into a smaller ball. "I don't believe it."

"It's true!"

"No, I believe it happened. I just can't believe it happened to you first!"

"Why not?" Sam asks, all offended.

"You and Molly are, like, the two biggest Goody

Two-Shoes in school, and now she's slipping you the tongue!"

"Don't say it like that! You make it sound so cheap."

"Cheap?" Ryan laughs.

"Leave him alone," I say. "I'm happy for you, Sam."

"Thank you, Noah. At least you still know how to be a good friend."

"What's *that* supposed to mean?" Ryan asks.

"What do you think? You're always so mean to me. It's a little tiring. It's like your main goal in life is to yuck my yummies."

Ryan stands up. "'Yuck my yummies'? Are you kidding me?"

"Guys," I say. "Stop fighting."

"It's a saying," Sam says. "And you do it. All the time."

"Well, excuse me for trying to help you!"

"Help me what?"

"Be a little less"—Ryan struggles with how to answer—"Sam-like!"

"What the heck is that supposed to mean!"

"Never mind!" Ryan stomps up the stairs and goes inside.

"Hey!" Sam says. He goes after Ryan, leaving me on the icy steps.

I finish my trail mix with frozen fingers—peanut, raisin, M&M, sunflower seed—feeling more alone than I've ever felt in my life.

After school, I see Mrs. Lewis waiting in the parking lot as soon as I step outside. Harper is already bounding down the steps to claim shotgun. Like I care.

"Hey, Noah," Mrs. Lewis says when I climb into the backseat. "School OK?"

"Yeah," I say.

Harper turns up the radio, and we drive to the high school for Stu. I wonder if she came for us first this time to rescue me as quickly as possible. I wonder if she knew I needed it.

When we pull into the high-school pickup area, I automatically look for Emma, and then remember she's not here. I watch as her friends filter outside, laughing and talking, hugging one another good-bye. No one seems to notice Emma isn't there. They don't act like something bad has happened. Like Emma is missing. Someone comes up behind Stu as he's walking out and jumps on his back for a piggyback ride. They sway and topple over, laughing. Stu is still chuckling when he gets to the car and finds Harper in the front seat.

"Out," he says through the window.

Harper locks the door and grins.

Stu pounds on the glass, and Mrs. Lewis yells at him to just get in the back.

When he sits next to me, he stops grinning. "Oh, hi, Noah. Any news about Emma?"

"No," I say. And if there was, I wouldn't tell him. I wouldn't tell any of these jerks.

I am 99 percent sure Stu was on Emma's *Lord of the Flies* list as one who would follow the beast. I'd add Harper, too. Jerks.

Stu puts his earbuds in and taps his thighs to the music no one else can hear. Harper stares out the window, bored. Mrs. Lewis sighs about one hundred and thirty times. I want to tell her to turn on the radio to end the silence, but I don't. I just sigh, too, and stare out the window like Harper, wishing this stupid car could go faster.

17

"Remember, try to be cheerful," my mom says for the third time since we got in the car. "The doctor says it's important for Emma to see that we're doing OK. We need to show Emma we're still carrying on and that we can't wait until she gets home. But not to make her feel guilty about being away. So . . . we have to be cheerful," she says again.

My dad taps the steering wheel in his nervous, anxious way.

I glance over at the small pile of presents we took from under the tree. The rest are still there, unopened.

No one remembered to water the tree, so a whole pile of needles slid off onto the packages when my mom reached under to get some for Emma. We were going to keep the tree up until Emma got home, but now it turns out we don't know exactly when that will be. Every so often an ornament drops off one of the sagging branches and rattles onto the floor, but no one bothers to pick those up, either. So the presents under the tree are covered in needles and ornaments and lost hope. And everyone pretends not to notice.

I pull out my copy of *A Separate Peace* and try not to get even more depressed, but it's hard. The last thing I want to read about right now is messed-up friendships, especially with Ryan and Sam fighting so much. At least I don't think it's so bad that one of them would push the other out of a tree . . . yet. I try reading for a while but it makes me carsick, so I drop the book on the seat and close my eyes and listen to the *click, click, click* of my mom's knitting needles coming from the front seat. She's working on a scarf for Emma, even though she probably won't be able to leave it there, which my dad points out just before we arrive.

"I know that," my mom says resentfully. "It's for when she comes home."

"I was just saying," my dad says, just as resentfully.

The building we arrive at is like an old house. Not at all what I was expecting. I thought it would look more like a hospital. Or a prison.

Instead, it's one of those tall Victorian houses I've really only seen on TV. We find a place to park along the street and go inside. The hallway has a black-and-white checked floor, and there's a big wooden desk with an old lady sitting at it.

"Good morning!" she says loudly.

We all force ourselves to smile at her, even though it hurts.

"We're here to see our daughter, Emma," my mom explains.

"What a sweet girl," the lady says, smiling.

My mom nods and starts to cry.

It's weird to think that this stranger knows my sister. Knows her enough to know she is a sweet girl.

The lady gets up and hands my mom a tissue. She pats her arm and says, "There, there." I didn't know people really still said that.

She leads us to a parlor and explains that this is where we get to visit. Then she tells us to wait there while she goes and gets Emma.

My dad paces around the room in his nervous way while my mom sits in an armchair and wipes her face.

"Get it together," my dad tells her. "We're supposed to be cheerful, remember? Positive? She can't see you like this."

But just as he's saying that, Emma walks in.

Since no one else seems to know what to do, I get up and hug her. I expect her to give me her usual punch first, but she squeezes me tight.

"How's Puker Prison?" I whisper in her ear.

"I miss you," she whispers back, instead of answering.

I'm afraid to look at her. To hug back too much, because I don't want to feel how small she is.

When I let go and we face each other again, though, I think she actually looks OK. She smiles, and it's a real smile, not forced-seeming. I guess for some reason I was expecting her to be wearing her hospital clothes, but she's wearing normal ones. Not her SpongeBob ensemble, just regular jeans and a normal sweater. One, not three.

Our hug seemed to break my parents' frozen stance, and they come over and hug her at the same time. Then we all sit down.

"You can stop looking at me like I'm dying," Emma says. "I'm OK."

"We just miss you—" my mom starts, then cries, forgetting all the rules.

"I'm sorry," Emma says.

"We just want you to get well," my dad says. "Whatever it takes." He gives my mom a look like, *Nice play.* She ignores him.

Emma tells us about her daily routine and how strict they are about things, but how everyone is pretty nice. She feels almost *too* positive about the place, and I get this uneasy feeling, like she's really not being herself after all. I think about the pep talk in the car and wonder if Emma's the one acting all cheerful and positive for *us.* I wish I could be alone with her so I could ask her what the real deal is, but obviously my parents aren't going to give up a second of their time with her, and we only have thirty minutes. So instead, Emma opens her Christmas presents and everyone tries to make chitchat, but it's totally awkward and uncomfortable. When Emma gets to my present, she takes a really long time to carefully remove the tape from the wrapping because I used paper I drew pictures on. The entire wrapping paper is little drawings I made of the Captain in different poses. As she picks back the tape with her chewed-to-the-nub fingernails, Emma starts to cry.

My parents look at me worriedly, like they are afraid whatever's inside is going to make her cry even worse. I can't really reassure them, but it bugs me that instead of even noticing all my hard work, they're focused on Emma. I mean, of course they are. But . . . I wish for once, just once, instead of paying every last bit of attention to her, they could notice what I made, what I can do.

"Careful," I say, when Emma pulls the paper off the box and starts to open it. "It's breakable."

She nods and removes the tissue I stuffed all around the present. Then she smiles and lifts out the piece I made for her.

"The glaze came out a little too dark," I say.

"No, it's perfect. I love it, Noah," she says. "Look what Noah made, you guys." She holds up my sculpture of the Captain to my parents. "Look how talented he is."

My parents smile and look a little surprised. "Wow, Noah!" my mom says. "That's really stunning!"

Emma hands it over so they can look more closely,

then gets up to hug me. "Thank you, brother," she says. "I'm sorry I've been such a jerk."

"Just get well," I say.

She lets go and sits back down. I wish she'd said, "OK." Or hugged me harder. Or anything to make me believe she'll try.

When our time is up, the old lady comes to get Emma. When it's my turn for a hug good-bye, she whispers in my ear again.

"I'll be OK. Promise."

But I don't know if I believe her.

The doctor we met at the hospital comes out next and takes my parents to her office, leaving me alone in the parlor. I listen hard for any sounds coming from the rest of the house, but it's eerily silent, and I wonder what Emma's doing now.

She said she gets to watch a little TV but mostly reads and spends time in therapy. She has to do stuff like go to the bathroom with the door open so she can't make herself throw up. My mom cringed when she told us. But Emma seemed to act like it was normal. Which only made it worse, I think.

My dad gave my mom a funny look.

"It's OK, Dad," Emma said. "It's good. I have to be honest about this."

Sometimes the truth hurts even more than the lies.

When my parents get back, they actually look a little more hopeful. They're even holding hands. We say good-bye to the old lady and then get in the car to go home. I fall asleep before we even reach the highway. It's the only way to survive being in the car with my parents again so soon.

I wake up when my phone buzzes in my pocket. I have a text from Ryan saying he got in a huge fight with Sam and they aren't speaking.

I don't reply.

A few minutes later, I get a text from Sam saying the same thing.

I don't reply.

My mom is knitting again.

My dad is tapping the steering wheel anxiously.

I text Emma, even though she isn't allowed to have a phone there.

It was good to see you, I write. *Hope you can come home soon.*

But instead of hitting send, I delete it. It's better than getting a bounce-back message saying DELIVERY FAILED.

At home, we get out of the car, go inside, and ignore one another as usual. I go up to my room and get into bed. I let the Captain jump up and lie next to me. I don't know why I'm so tired all the time, but all I want to do is sleep. All I want to do is drift off and not come back until I can wake up and have everything be back to normal. Instead, it seems like every time I wake up, things are worse.

After ten minutes of lying there, someone knocks on my door. I don't answer. It opens anyway.

"Noah," my dad says, "why are you in bed? It's only seven o'clock. And why is the dog on the bed when you know that's against the rules?"

"I'm tired," I say. "And it's a dumb rule."

My dad sighs. "Get out of there and come down. Mom and I want to talk to you."

"But—"

"Please."

"Give me five minutes."

"Fine."

I wait for him to leave, then roll over on my back and look up at my boring ceiling like always. Whatever they want, it can't be good. They're probably going to make me see a therapist to make sure Emma's illness hasn't affected me in some devastating way. *Don't worry, Mom and Dad, I still fit into my husky jeans just fine.*

I drag myself out of bed and go downstairs. The Captain doesn't bother to leave his spot on the bed.

At the last step, I stop. All the lights in the living room are off except for the lights on the tree.

"Merry Christmas," my dad says.

Our stockings are draped on various chairs, just like they should have been two weeks ago.

"Sorry it took so long," my mom says.

"Shouldn't we wait for Emma?" I ask.

My parents exchange a look.

"She won't be home for a while," my dad says.

"What do you mean? How long?"

"They'll reevaluate in a few weeks."

"But—I thought she'd be home in a few weeks."

"We know," my mom says. "It feels like forever. But we can visit every weekend. And this way, they can get her in a really stable, healthy place. That's the best defense. She needs to be away from . . . her triggers . . . until she can get well. Really well."

"Triggers?"

"The things that make her want to . . . that could cause a relapse."

"Well, what are they?"

My mom and dad exchange looks again.

"Us? Are we her triggers?" *Am I?*

"It's complicated, honey," my mom says.

"C'mon," my dad says. "Open your stocking. Emma would want you to."

We go to our stockings and sit down. Emma's stocking is still hanging on the hook at the mantel, empty. I wonder if they'll stuff it before she comes home, or if they'll forget. I tell myself I'll do it. I'll put all her favorite things in it. Warm socks, Chapstick, watermelon Jolly Ranchers . . .

"You go first, Noah," my mom says.

I pull out a chocolate Santa. Then it's my dad's turn, and he does the same. Then my mom. Next I get a deck of cards. More chocolate. Gummy bears. Silly Putty. The same stuff they give me every year, no matter how old I get.

When we finish our stockings, we start opening

presents. My mom plays elf and selects gifts from under the tree. I didn't notice until now, but there's Christmas music playing quietly on the stereo. Every so often, my mom pushes a box aside into a growing pile for Emma.

It's quiet and sad, opening presents. We say thank you and act all grateful and a little surprised each time we open something, but without Emma, it feels wrong to be doing this.

"Here," my dad says, handing me another present. "Emma told me she didn't want you to wait for her to come home before you open it."

"But—"

"Open it, honey," my mom says. "Emma asked to make sure you did."

It's a huge box wrapped in the colored-paper cartoons that get printed only on Sundays. She must have saved them for a few weeks to have enough to cover the whole box.

Inside the box are a bunch more boxes, all wrapped the same way.

The first is really heavy, and inside is a bag of pottery clay. The other boxes each have a different sculpting tool. Most we have at school, but some I've never seen before. I wonder if Ms. Cliff told Emma about my art. How else would Emma know what I've been up to?

The final box has a tiny vest in it that Emma crocheted for Curly. It's soft and smells like Emma's perfume. I picture her at the treatment center again, all alone, and Curly at the animal hospital, all confused and sick because of me.

"Are you OK?" my dad asks. He reaches over and puts his hand on my knee.

"Yeah," I say. "I just wish she was here."

We finish opening our gifts and then separate all the paper and boxes for recycling, and then my mom says she's tired and can we get takeout for dinner. My dad says that's a great idea, so that's what we do, and then we watch *A Christmas Story,* which we always do on Christmas night. But it doesn't feel the same without Emma snorting at all the punch lines. And because it's not Christmas anymore. And because everything basically feels like a big lie.

"We'll take the tree down tomorrow," my mom says before going upstairs to bed.

I feel terrible for thinking it, but I really hope she doesn't ask me to help.

18

Please Do Not Abuse the Suggestion Box

"Noah!" The Tank waves me over to his room on Monday morning. Inside, Curly is sitting on his desk wearing her old Santa suit. She chirps when she sees me.

"Is she OK?" I ask.

"Good as new. Though I don't know if she's wild about today's outfit."

I slip my backpack off my shoulder and dig inside for Emma's vest.

I hand it to the Tank.

"Aw, that's nice," he says. "So soft."

"Emma made it," I say.

He seems to catch his breath like he's trying not to cry. "That's real sweet," he says. "You went to visit her this weekend, right? How's she doing?"

I shrug. "She's OK, I guess."

He puts his giant hand on my shoulder and squeezes. It makes me need to cry, but I manage to hold it in.

"Let's switch her up," he says, to change the subject.

Curly looks relieved when he takes off the red-and-white suit and replaces it with Emma's vest. She rubs her face against my hand and purrs.

"I guess she forgives me," I say.

"Of course she does! It wasn't your fault she did something stupid. She's just not the sharpest knife in the drawer. Damn cat eats anything. No worries, all right?"

"All right."

"Where's Curly's Santa suit?" Lily asks when she and the other students come to class. "She looked so cute!"

"It was chafing," the Tanks says, and winks at me. "Besides, it's time to put that away until next year."

"That's a cute vest. Is it new?"

"Emma made it for her," I say.

"Oh."

She's quiet for a minute. "I heard what happened, Noah. I'm really sorry."

"Thanks."

She hugs me awkwardly just as Sam and Ryan, who appear to have made up, walk in. Sam looks thrilled to see me in the arms of a girl, but Ryan looks like I just stabbed him in the back. What is *with* him?

We all find our seats. Sam keeps elbowing me and grinning.

"Really, no," I say. But he keeps on about it, and honestly I just feel like punching him, because there is more to life than having a girlfriend and I can tell it's driving Ryan crazy and I just want to go home and go to bed and not have to deal with anyone.

Curly walks around our feet, purring happily.

At lunch, I go to the Community Room, since it's too cold to go outside. Sam and Molly squish together on one of the couches and attempt to eat one-handed so they can hold hands. Ryan keeps looking over at them and shaking his head in disgust.

"What?" Sam finally says.

"Huh?" Ryan acts like he doesn't know what Sam means.

"What's your problem?" Sam asks.

"Nothing."

"Then stop doing that."

"Doing what?" Ryan asks.

"Looking at us and shaking your head!"

"I wasn't!"

"Yes, you were!"

Everyone else in the room stops talking.

"Maybe if you weren't so grumpy all the time, you could have a girlfriend, too!" Sam yells.

Ryan's face turns beet red. "Shut up, Sam."

"No!"

So much for them making up.

Molly slips her hand out of Sam's.

"All you do is mope around and make mean comments under your breath."

"Well, all *you* do is fall all over Molly every second. It's embarrassing!"

"For who?"

"It should be for *you*!"

"You're just jealous."

"Right."

Molly makes this hurt expression and walks away. Sam gets up to go after her, then stops.

"You're a real jerk, you know that?"

"*I* didn't do anything," Ryan says.

I am so tired of the two of them fighting over stupid stuff.

"Will you both just *shut up?*" I yell. I toss my lunch bag aside and stand up.

Everyone looks at me, mouths dropped.

"What the heck, Noah?" Ryan says.

"I'm sick of this!" I shout in his face.

"Me too," Sam says.

"I'm sick of you, too!" I bark at him. "You're no better! All you two do is bicker about meaningless stuff. And Sam, you constantly have to rub it in Ryan's face that you have a girlfriend!"

I hear the words coming out and I don't want to say them, but they keep spewing out of me anyway. It's like suddenly I'm the one with a beast inside, and it is encouraging me to let all the horrible thoughts and feelings I've ever had rage out of me.

"I'm so tired of you two! You don't care about anything important! All you care about is your stupid, meaningless problems! There's more to life, but you don't even see it! You're too busy being jerks to each other over nothing! Like who has a stupid girlfriend! It's pathetic!"

As if that's not enough, I push Sam out of the way and he stumbles backward into Ryan. I can feel everyone's eyes on me. Shocked eyes. This is not a Noah thing to do. Noah is quiet. Noah (mostly) follows the rules. Noah doesn't make waves. Noah is *never* violent.

Well, today, Noah feels like causing a tsunami. The beast is here.

"I'm done with everyone!" I yell. The Suggestion Box catches my eye, and I walk over and push it to the floor. The top pops off and a few strips of paper fall out. "All your stupid complaints are ridiculous!" I yell. "Don't you get that there are more important things happening in the world? All you care about is what the girls wear and whether Secret Santas are offensive. Who cares!"

I stomp out of the room, then race down the hall

and out the door. It's freezing, of course. School won't be out for another hour, and even as I'm rushing down the front steps, I know I'm going to be in serious trouble. I keep running anyway.

Not far away, there's an old general store, and I head for that. Maybe I can wander around in there to warm up and then somehow get my carpool ride without being seen in the school parking lot. I could come back and hide behind a car or something.

Before I cross the street to the store, I turn back to see if anyone followed me. No one did. I admit, I'm a little disappointed that no one even tried.

I walk more slowly to the store, just in case. But no one catches up.

Inside, the store smells like pine needles. All touristy stores in Vermont seem to smell like this. I walk down an aisle of overpriced maple-syrup products.

"Can I help you with anything, sweetie?" a lady asks. She's using a feather duster to clean the jars on a shelf at the end of the aisle.

"No, thanks, just looking," I say. That probably sounds weird coming from someone like me. I don't exactly look like a tourist shopping for maple products.

"Shouldn't you be in school?" she asks, checking her watch.

I shrug and turn to go down the next aisle and almost run into the Tank. I guess someone followed me after all.

"Noah," he says, all out of breath. "You need to come back to school now."

"I don't want to," I say.

He puts his hand on my shoulder in a firm way, but gentle, too. "That's not really a good enough reason for me to let you stay here."

The woman peeks around the corner with her duster. "Everything OK?"

The Tank nods at her. "Yeah, Shannon. No worries."

She smiles. "Nice to see you," she says. I think she's blushing.

"C'mon," the Tank says. "Let's get back."

"Do I really have to?"

He studies me.

"Why don't you want to?"

"I'm just . . . really tired."

"What, were you going to take a nap here or something? I don't see what 'tired' has to do with you dashing out of school and coming to shop for souvenirs."

"I mean I'm tired of everyone. At school. I'm tired of how they all act."

"How do they act?"

"Like nothing happened. Like nothing *is* happening. Like they don't care."

"About Emma?"

I don't answer.

"I know you're going through a hard time, Noah. But running out of school is only going to make things worse. What you did with the Suggestion Box didn't help, either."

"But that thing is so stupid!"

"Why do you say that?"

"No one puts anything serious in there. It's a total joke."

"What would you put in there?" he asks.

"I don't know." I picture myself swiping the box onto the floor and the looks everyone gave me.

"Try. Give me a suggestion."

"I wish people would spend more energy on stuff that actually matters," I say.

"That's a good one. I think I'll suggest that. What kind of stuff do you think matters?"

"I don't know. Just . . . *doing* something instead

of complaining all the time. I don't get the point." I think about Emma and how it seems like all the stuff in her life, everything she's interested in, always has a purpose. Like her message-y music, and all her rules about what we could and couldn't eat. Only now I realize maybe those things ended up having a bad purpose. Maybe they were all part of her terrible journey to Puker Prison.

"The Complaint Box is mostly just for fun," the Tank says. "To give us something to talk about, and maybe laugh about, during Community Meeting. But if you think we should take it more seriously, we can try."

"It doesn't matter," I say. "Just forget it."

He picks up a little pine-scented pillow and sniffs it, then puts it down again.

"It sucks when you're hurting and life just keeps going on around you. I get that. But there needs to be room for fun, too. What's the point of life if you can't enjoy it?"

I shrug.

"C'mon," he says. "Let's get you back to school."

"Do I really have to go back? No one will even notice I'm missing."

"Trust me, people will notice. With that exit of

yours, I'm pretty sure everyone is wondering where you went."

"Maybe they wonder, but they don't care."

"I care. Why do you think I'm here?"

I shrug again. "Because it's your job?"

He gets an annoyed look on his face. "You really believe that? Fine. Suit yourself. Stay here if you want."

He turns around and walks down the aisle without me.

He should be dragging me back. He should be slinging me over his shoulder and carrying me. He should be asking me, "What's wrong, Noah? What's *really* wrong?" But instead, he walks away.

The bell above the door tinkles when he opens it and lets it swing shut. Then the store is quiet.

The woman with the feather duster peeks around the corner again but lets me be.

For the next hour, I walk aimlessly up and down the aisles, reading the prices on different-shaped maple-sugar candy and pine-scented pillows. My chest feels heavy and empty at the same time, and I realize this is what true loneliness feels like. Like you're full of hurt but completely hollowed out all at once. I wonder if this is how Emma feels, away from everyone she knows. Or if she felt this way before she left. I wonder if this is how Ryan feels, and why he acts like such a jerk sometimes. All I know is that it feels awful. And the worst part is, I can't really imagine this feeling ever going away.

19

Please Try to Spend More Energy on Stuff That Matters

I slip into Mrs. Lewis's car as soon as she pulls into the parking lot and before anyone can see where I've been hiding, crouched behind the Tank's truck.

"Noah! Where did you come from?"

I don't tell her.

"You should sit up front! You finally beat Harper!"

"That's OK," I say, buckling myself into the backseat and slouching low so no one will see me.

The car is toasty warm. I lean back and let my frozen hands start to defrost. They sting and ache as they warm up.

"Where've you been?" Harper asks when he gets in the front.

I blow on my hands instead of answering.

When he turns back to demand an answer, I scowl at him.

"You're so weird," he says.

"Harper! Don't be rude!" Mrs. Lewis looks horrified.

"Whatever." He starts drumming his fingers on the dashboard. "If anyone else skipped out of school, they'd get in trouble," he says in a whiny voice. "But just because your sister—"

"Harper!" his mom yells again. "What is *wrong* with you?" She looks at me in the rearview mirror. "Noah, are you OK?" she asks.

I nod like any liar would.

"Sorry," Harper says. But I can tell he's not.

"You sure you're OK?" his mom asks.

I nod again and lean my head against the window so I'm out of her view in the mirror.

"I know you have a lot going on at home. Let us know if there's anything we can do, all right?"

I keep my eyes closed but murmur, "Thanks." I really don't know what she thinks she can do. She must know there's nothing anyone can do. There never is. Unless you tie someone down and force-feed them, what can you do? Pray therapy works? Pray for a miracle? But who are we supposed to pray to? That's what I want to know. God doesn't answer prayers. God lets bad things happen. Why hasn't everyone figured that out yet?

As soon as we pull into the pickup area at the high school, Sara runs over to our car and knocks on my window. I roll it down a little.

"Hey, Noah," she says. "Can you get this to Emma? All my texts are bouncing." She slides a letter through the slit in the window.

"Sure," I say.

"Have you talked to her recently?"

I can tell everyone in the car is listening by how quiet it got.

"Yeah," I say.

"Is she coming home soon?"

"I don't know."

"Well, tell her I said hi. OK?"

"Sure."

She looks sad as she steps back from the car, but someone comes up behind her and hugs her and she turns around and laughs, and they practically skip toward the waiting area. What a fake.

Stu finally comes out and gets in the car, and no one talks all the way to my house as usual.

"Bye, Noah," Mrs. Lewis says when I unbuckle my seat belt. Her voice is full of concern and kindness.

"Thanks for the ride," I say, because that's what we all say when we get out of the carpool car. *Thanks for the ride.* And thanks for not asking me any more questions. And thanks for not acting like nothing terrible has happened. Even though the ride was awkward, it felt like the first time I wasn't the only one who felt the missing piece.

As they drive off, I imagine what happens next. Mrs. Lewis will ask Harper what happened today and why I wasn't in school. But that will last two minutes before she asks them both how much homework they have. Then they'll go home and she'll make them dinner, which they will all scarf down and keep down. They'll probably sit around and laugh about something stupid and unimportant, and no one will give Emma or me another thought. Because for everyone else, life goes on. Nothing has changed for them, so why should they act any different?

* * *

I go inside and find my dad vacuuming the living room. He turns the machine off when he sees me.

"Hey, Noah!" he calls, all cheery. "How was your day?"

I shrug.

"We heard from Emma's doctor today, and she's doing really well! If she stays on track, she'll come home by February break."

"I thought she'd be home sooner than *that*," I say.

He stops smiling as his enthusiasm drains out of him. "Try to be positive, Noah. It's good news. I promise."

"It doesn't sound like good news."

"Some kids have to stay there for two months or even longer."

"Oh."

His smile comes back. "So, see? This is good!"

"Why are you home?" I ask.

"I couldn't concentrate at work. I thought I'd come home and clean this place up. We've really let things go."

I look around and notice just how dirty and dusty

everything has gotten. How it smells stale and not like our house anymore. The sun shines through the window, but it doesn't *feel* sunny. It feels sad.

The Captain wanders into the room and wags his tail at me. He stretches his head out for a pat and licks my hand.

"Don't you go shedding all over my clean rug, stinkpot," my dad says.

The Captain wags his tail harder when anyone talks to him, so he starts wagging like nuts, and you can actually see strands of fur launching off his body and dancing through the air.

"Put him outside, would you, Noah? And then why don't you grab a rag and help with some dusting."

That was always Emma's job. I mop the kitchen and bathroom; Dad vacuums the rugs; Emma dusts.

"I have a ton of homework," I say. "Couldn't I just take the Captain up with me?"

The lie makes my chest hurt.

"Oh. Sure. You should do that, then." The last of his enthusiasm and hope drain back out of his face, and I feel terrible and satisfied at the same time.

We have to live like this until February break, and he's happy? What if I can't last that long? What if the thought of getting in the carpool without Emma one more day makes me want to run away for good?

Why doesn't anyone understand how hard it is?

I leave my dad standing in the living room, looking lost and confused. It seems I leave everyone looking like that lately.

"C'mon, stinky," I say to the Captain.

In my room, I kick off my shoes and drop my backpack on the floor. Then I crawl into bed and pull the covers over my head. My sheets smell gross. I don't know how long it's been since they've been washed, but definitely too long. Laundry is just another thing that stopped when Emma left.

I close my eyes and try not to think about how she looked when we saw her. Scared and small. But of course when I think of her, that's what I see. That and all the other things I don't want to remember. My parents pounding on the bathroom door. The worried look on my dad's face when Emma pushed her food around on her plate. My mom nervously pacing when Emma would disappear in the bathroom for a minute too long. Sam and Ryan whispering about how tiny she felt when Sam danced with her but that he didn't have the guts to tell me.

We all knew, didn't we?

We all knew something was wrong again.

So why didn't we try harder to stop it?

I know it's not really our fault. That we can't force Emma to eat. My parents can make her see the therapist more, but what else? I don't know. She can't stay at the treatment center forever. And that's why it's so scary.

I sink deeper down into my bed and put my pillow over my head. I feel my eyes wanting to cry, but nothing comes out. The vacuum comes back on downstairs. The Captain jumps onto my bed and walks in a circle before collapsing on my feet. He lets out a quiet whistler. I shove him a little, but he just thumps his tail, the stinker. I wonder if he knew, too. I wonder if he sensed something was wrong.

I breathe in my stale sheets and listen to the steady hum of the vacuum until the sound puts me to sleep.

I wake to a hand shaking me.

"Noah, Noah," my mom says gently. I must have slept for a while if my mom is home from work.

"It's time for dinner. Are you OK?" She pulls the blankets off my head, and I squint up at her. She looks pale and tired. She puts her hand on my forehead.

"You don't feel feverish."

"I'm just tired," I say.

She sits on my bed and stares at the floor.

"Ms. Cliff called, honey. She told me about what happened today."

"Oh."

"Do you want to tell me your version?"

"Not really."

I roll over under the covers again. It feels weird to be in bed with my clothes on. It's hot, and hard to move.

"I know this is hard," my mom says. "Being worried about Emma all the time and not knowing when she's coming home—"

"Dad said she might come home in February."

"Well, that's what they said today. As long as she stays on track."

I'm beginning to really hate that phrase. *On track.* It's like we're all supposed to stay on some boring path toward a goal someone else made for us. I'm sure that's how Emma feels. But in her case, I'm glad she's being forced to stay on it. I wish her own path wasn't so messed up and dangerous.

"What if she doesn't?" I ask. I think of the words

to "Free Bird" again and how Emma sang it, like it was her own personal anthem. What if she *can't* change?

"Doesn't what?" my mom asks.

"You know. Stay on track?"

I turn my head back so I can see her face when she answers.

"She has to," my mom says. Her bottom lip quivers. She pats my legs. "Scoot these up, would you?"

I bend my knees, and she slides herself across the bed so she can lean against the wall. She reaches for my legs over the covers and squeezes. The Captain makes a noise from the floor. He must have jumped down when I was sleeping.

"Don't even think about it," my mom says to him. "I can see you've already been up here, you bad dog."

"It's not his fault. I let him."

"I wish you wouldn't. Your comforter needs to get washed now."

"Sorry."

She squeezes my legs tighter.

"I wish I understood why she does it," I say.

"Me too, honey."

She closes her eyes and takes a long, slow breath. This is her method for keeping from crying.

"You can't run away from school again, Noah."

"I know."

"It's not fair for me to say this, but I'm going to anyway. I can't be worried about you on top of everything going on with Emma. I just don't know if this heart of mine can take any more worry."

"I'm sorry," I say.

"I know it's hard for you to be at school. But you've gotta go. It's just the way it is."

"I hate it there."

A tear escapes her no-cry method, and she quickly wipes it away. "I'm sorry."

"Everyone acts like nothing's wrong. Like the biggest problem in the world is what's in their lunch bag. I can't stand it. No one cares about Emma. Or me. Or what's happening."

"Of course they care."

"Well, they don't act like it—that's for sure."

"Life goes on, I guess, when you're not directly affected."

"It's hard to watch—that's all. It's hard to listen to them. Every time someone complains about something stupid, I want to say, 'At least your sister isn't so sick she's in some hospital being force-fed!' I'm so tired of their stupid problems."

My mom sighs and pats my leg again. "I know, honey. It's the same for me at work. I hate going in. I hate the sympathetic looks that have stopped seeming sincere. I want this to be over and have Emma back as much as you do, believe me."

"Do you ever want to yell at them? Your co-workers?"

"Sure. All the time. When I overhear someone complaining about their kids doing some mundane thing, I want to say the same things you do. But I don't, Noah. Because it's not their fault. They're behaving like normal people. It's just that our life right now isn't in sync with anyone else's. But some-times, yeah. I want to scream at them and tell them I'd give my right hand to have the worst thing wrong with my kid be that she doesn't make her bed in the morning."

We hear my dad coming up the stairs, and my mom sighs again, like she's really tired.

"Hey, guys," he says when he steps through the doorway. "Any room on there for me?"

My mom pats the bed beside her, and I curl up in a smaller ball.

"Dinner's ready when you are," he says. But none of us get up. For a long time, we don't even say anything. We just sit on my bed, like it's a tiny island or a boat. It feels sad but good at the same time. Good to have them here with me. Recognizing that I'm here and hurting, too. I feel like my bed-boat is completely out to sea and we don't have a paddle. We're just drifting silently. And maybe it's OK. Maybe it's Emma we're waiting for, to rescue us. She's supposed to be the strong one. She's always been the true captain of our ship. I understand now why we all seem so lost without her, besides the obvious part of being worried about her. We've always relied on her. She's the one who calls the shots in this family. She's the one who gets us all to go to the movies or for a lame family walk or to try making new meals for dinner or to change the color of the walls in the living room. She's the one who's full of life, pulling us along after her. Without Emma, we're lost. Alone. And maybe that's our fault. Maybe we depended on her too much.

I force myself to sit up. When I pull the covers off, I feel cold and exposed but more awake.

"We should eat," I say.

My parents look at me like they've never heard my voice before. But really it's just that they've never heard me take charge before.

I get out of bed and pull my covers up in a half-hearted attempt to make it. My mom smiles appreciatively, and I know she's probably thinking about her co-worker's daughter.

I reach for her hand and pull her up. Then we all go downstairs, the Captain following behind.

Dinner is pizza delivered from our old favorite place before Emma went vegan and there wasn't anything on the menu she would eat. I help my mom set the table, and my dad pours us all soda, which we rarely have, and certainly not without a comment from Emma telling us how much sugar and other bad ingredients it has.

We eat slowly. The tomato sauce and cheese taste stronger than I remember. Sweet and salty. The root beer bubbles sting my tongue. Everything tastes different, and I savor it. The forbidden, greasy cheese. The second glass of root beer. My parents eating food they've probably been craving just as much as I have but were always too afraid to eat in front of Emma in case it made her lose her appetite, which is the excuse she always gave.

Every so often, I look at Emma's empty place and feel guilty. But at the same time, it feels so good to fill my body up with food. To eat until I'm full. I try to imagine Emma enjoying this feeling. I make a silent wish that someday she will. Someday she'll want to pig out with me and not want to make herself sick after. Someday, she'll be normal again. *Please let her just be normal again. I'll make her bed for the rest of her life if she'll just come home and be OK.*

But I have this horrible feeling that things will never be normal. As my parents and I eat pizza as if it's the last time we'll have a meal like this, I start to feel sick to my stomach. All the salty greasy cheese that tasted so good five minutes ago suddenly feels like it's choking me.

"Do you want another slice, Noah?" my dad asks. "There's still plenty more."

The way he looks at me, like he is begging me to eat and enjoy it, makes me force myself to take another slice. I force myself to smile as I chew what now tastes disgusting to me. I do it for them, because I can tell watching me eat this forbidden food is making them feel something they need to feel, even if I don't know what that is.

As I chew, I look at Emma's empty chair again and start to hate her. To hate her and miss her and love her all at the same time. As I do, I feel all that cheese and sauce and pizza crust churning in my stomach, begging me to let it all out. But I know if that happened, if I threw up now, it would destroy my parents. So I take another sip of soda, swallow it down, and pretend that this is the best meal I've had in ages.

20

Please Don't Take Your Bad Day Out on Innocent People

Ryan and Sam ignore me the next day at school. In fact, no one really talks to me. They all kind of look at me and back off, like I could explode again at any minute. Fine. I'd rather be left alone anyway.

In art, I get some clay and work at a table by myself. No one asks what I'm working on. Not even Ms. Cliff. I have this strange feeling that they all secretly decided that no one should bother me. I try to shut everything out but the clay in my hands, how it feels cold and hard at first but then softens as I work it, slowly shaping nothing into something. It doesn't matter what.

Every so often, I catch Ms. Cliff watching me out of the corner of her eye, as if she can't help herself. But she manages not to ask me how I'm doing or tell me I should come to chat in her office.

Even the Tank leaves me alone in class.

The only one who doesn't seem to have gotten the Don't Talk to Noah memo is Curly. She follows me around like a puppy would, rubbing against my legs and sitting on my lap from class to class. Sometimes I think she knows when someone needs a friend. Not that I need a friend. At least, not the kind of friends who talk nonstop about nothing. I'm really starting to understand Emma's list of beasts and why she made it. Doesn't anyone care about stuff besides who broke up with who and who has crappy taste in music and who probably cheated on the French quiz? If I had to make a list today, I think they'd all be on there. But maybe that makes me a beast, too.

At lunch, I sit by myself until Lily comes over and gives me a disapproving look.

"Way to go, Noah. I hope you're satisfied," she says before stomping off.

I have no idea what she's talking about, and I don't

really care. But then Belle storms over to me and waits for me to look up.

"Did you hear?" she asks, all know-it-all-ish.

"What?"

"Molly and Sam broke up."

"And?"

"Good going," she says. "I always thought you were nice, but I was so wrong."

"What do I have to do with it?" I ask.

"Your little outburst made them get in a fight."

"Why?"

She looks at me like I'm an idiot.

"Because of all the things you said. Molly thought you were a jerk, and Sam stood up for you, and then they both started arguing, and then they broke up."

Curly comes over and rubs against my leg.

"Sam stood up for me?"

"Of course, stupid. Aren't you best friends?"

I don't know what to say.

"Don't ask me why," she adds. "You said some pretty mean things. I hope you're proud."

"I'm not. I was just . . . really mad."

"No kidding."

"Whatever," I say.

"Great attitude." She looks at me like I'm a rat. I think about the kid who doesn't make her bed and imagine that's Belle. I want to yell at her and tell her how unimportant and stupid Sam and Molly's relationship is, but instead I pet Curly and ignore her.

"Just because your sister is sick doesn't mean it's OK to act like a jerk," she says before walking away.

"What does she know?" I ask Curly quietly.

Curly licks my hand and walks away, too.

After school when I go up to my room, there's a letter on my messy-but-made bed from Emma. My dad must have put it there. I can hear him in the kitchen making dinner, which means he left work early again. I hope he doesn't get fired.

I sit in the beanbag chair Emma gave me and listen to the beads settle in their comforting way. The envelope is decorated with little peace signs and funny faces. I take my time checking out each face, trying to see if the people are supposed to be anyone I know, or just random. One has glasses, and I think that's Sam. One is pouting, and I tell myself that's Ryan, not me. I try to imagine Emma at the treatment place, sitting at some unfamiliar desk or table, decorating this envelope for me. I wonder what she was thinking about. I wonder if she was missing me — us — and wanting to come home.

I turn the letter over and over before I finally get the nerve to open it. I don't know why I'm scared. I just somehow know that inside, I could find the real Emma or the pretending Emma. The one who tells the truth or the one who lies. My sister or the demon that took over her soul. What if I can't tell the difference?

Slowly, I tear the envelope open and slide out the neatly folded paper inside. At the top, she's written my name in cute bubble letters in different colors.

Dear Noah,

    I miss you!

    I've been here for what feels like a pretty long time. I don't know how much longer I'll be here. A few more weeks at least, I guess. But I'll be home before you know it. What's it like to be an only child? Are Mom and Dad spoiling you?

    I'm sorry I ruined Christmas. And I suppose New Year's, too. I forgot to ask you about that when you visited. Was it boring having to hang out with Mom and Dad alone? Or did you break out and go to a New Year's party?

*It was pretty strange to be here and not
home. I pretended it was just another day,
even though the staff gave us hot chocolate
with candy canes for stirring it. Whoop-de-do.*
Just another day. *That's my new mantra. Do
you like it?*

*Anyway, I just wanted you to know I'm
thinking of you. And that I'm sorry. And that
I probably won't be home for a while, if you
want to know the truth.*

*But I'm trying. That's what I really want
you to know. That I'm trying really hard. Please
try to convince Mom and Dad of that. I know
they're scared.*

I love you,
Emma

P.S. Give the Captain a hug for me.
P.P.S. Remember: Just another day!

I read the note again, looking for any secret clues or
possible lies. I study all the decorations for hidden
meaning. The hearts. The smiley faces. The flowers.

Did she drink the hot chocolate? Did she eat the

candy cane? Is she still insisting on her vegan diet? Did she try to puke it all up anyway? Why did she call me an only child? Does she really think I would want that? She's trying, but does that mean she's succeeding?

I fold the paper and put it back in the envelope.

Food smells waft up from downstairs and make my stomach growl. I go to my desk and tear out a piece of paper from my social studies notebook.

DEAR EMMA, I write in block letters. Then I make shadows around the blocks and use my colored pencils to fill in the letters.

> *Thanks for writing. Please don't be sorry about Christmas and New Year's.*

Wait. Should I really say that? Don't I *want* her to feel sorry? I erase the sentence.

> *Christmas and New Year's weren't the same without you. Your stocking will be overflowing when you get home, waiting for you to open it. I promise it will have good stuff.*

I stop. I am terrible at writing letters. My mom makes me write thank-you notes to my grandparents whenever they send me presents, even though they're usually lame. But that's my only practice.

Carpool is so boring without you.

Will that make her feel guilty? Or like she needs to get better faster so she can come back and save me?

Sara gave me a letter to send to you and I put it in the mail. Did you get it?
I've been using the tools you sent me in art. Ms. Cliff said I could use them in class as long as I shared, but I'm the only one still working with clay.

Ugh. Would Emma really care about this? But I want her to know how much her present meant to me. I keep it.

I hope you get better and come home soon. Nothing is the same without you. It's all worse.

I start to erase the last sentence, then decide to keep it. It's the truth.

Love, Noah

I reread my note, then add decorations. I draw a stocking overflowing with presents with a speech bubble that says, "Emma, open me!" And myself, looking miserable in the carpool car. I make sure to draw Stu and Harper really exaggerated, with Harper's big nose and Stu's big head. I draw Curly with a Santa hat on. I draw the Captain farting under the Christmas tree. I try to fill every free space on the paper with something funny. Then I color everything in. I put it in an envelope and start to write the address from the letter Emma sent. It feels strange to write her name with the wrong address. It should be 10 Atkins Road, not this other place. This other city. I decide not to decorate the outside. I just can't.

"Noah! Dinner!" my dad calls.

I leave the envelope on my desk and go downstairs.

Dinner is lasagna, my old favorite. We haven't had it in ages. Not like this. With real ricotta instead of Emma's weird almond cheese that doesn't taste like cheese.

"Nothing like real cheese, huh?" my dad asks. It's the first time I've seen him smile without forcing it in a long time.

"Where's Mom?"

"She had a meeting. I thought we'd have a nice early dinner and then maybe watch a movie or something."

"Dad, it's a school night. I have homework."

He waves his hand. "You can do it later, can't you?"

"I guess."

"I just thought it would be nice to hang out. Just the two of us." He cuts a piece of lasagna and then passes me a basket filled with garlic bread. Everything smells delicious. The bread is slathered with real butter and sprinkled with parmesan cheese. When I take a bite, the flavors are almost too strong.

"This is amazing, Dad," I say, since he seems so excited about it.

My dad's mouth is full, but I can tell he's still smiling. He gives me a goofy thumbs-up.

We eat mostly without talking, stuffing our faces with cheese and pasta. But just like with the pizza, about halfway through the meal, everything starts to taste wrong. My stomach tightens. I put down my fork.

"What's wrong?" my dad asks.

"I think I ate too fast," I say.

"Drink some milk. You'll feel better."

I sip some milk and notice it's cow's milk, not soy.

I feel like I'm going to throw up.

"Hmm," my dad says. "Maybe you're just not used to all this dairy. Maybe we've all become lactose intolerant."

I don't know what that means, but I don't ask, because I'm pretty sure that's not what's wrong. I'm pretty sure what's wrong is that I feel guilty for eating things Emma is against. I feel guilty knowing that I can eat this and not feel like I have to punish myself for it after. I feel guilty because I'm here with my dad, and she's not. And it feels like by eating this stuff, we're being unfaithful to her. Like we're lying to her.

My dad puts down his fork, too. "I'm sorry, Noah. I should have asked if you were OK eating dairy. It was wrong to assume."

"It's fine," I say.

He looks at me like he knows it's not, though. "I wish I knew the right thing to do. I'm the parent. I should. But sometimes I really don't."

"It's all right, Dad."

He wipes his eyes with his napkin. "This is so hard."

"I know."

He puts his napkin next to his plate. "You go on up and do your homework. I'll take care of the dishes."

"What about watching a movie?" I ask.

He shakes his head. "Maybe later, kid."

"All right." I bring my plate to the kitchen and put it in the dishwasher. The Captain follows me in, and I let him lick the plates in the dishwasher before I close it. No one needs to know.

In my room, I check my phone for messages, out of habit. Of course there aren't any. I haven't had any for days. I scroll through some of the old ones and feel a twinge of missing Sam and Ryan and our stupid conversations. I wonder if they're still mad at each other. I wonder if they're having conversations without me now. I wish it was still fall and our biggest worry was going to the school dance and whether anyone would dance with us. Why did that seem so important? I can't remember.

I find Emma's letter and read it again. There's really nothing much there. No clue to say why she did what she did. Or does. I don't understand it. I've read all the stupid pamphlets they gave us at the place she's staying. All the websites they said to go to. But none of them really make sense. None of them tell me why. Why Emma? She's the good one. The perfect one. She's the popular one. The pretty one. Everyone wants to be her friend. She doesn't need to be anything different from what she already is, so why would she do this to herself? It's like she sabotaged her life. For what?

How could she be so stupid?

Doesn't she know how many people can only dream of looking like her? Of being as smart as her? Of being as loved as her?

How could she be so ungrateful? How could she put herself at so much risk?

How could she be so selfish?

I almost tear her letter in half but stop.

It's a disease, I tell myself. *It's not her fault. She doesn't want to be sick.*

OK.

Fine.

So whose fault *is* it?

21

To the People at This School Who Have Been Acting Depressed Lately: Don't Stop Believing

For the next few weeks, my life is kind of the same. Go to school. Ignore everyone. Be ignored back. Go home. Eat increasingly rich and cheesy and forbidden food made by my dad. Feel sick. Go to my room to do homework. Watch mindless TV. Write a letter to Emma. Wait for her to come say good night, even though I know she can't. Eventually fall asleep.

Every night at dinner, my mom gives my dad a funny look about what he's serving, but she never tells him to stop. We have baked mac and cheese. Mashed potatoes with real butter ponds. Homemade pizza.

More lasagna. The only rule we don't break is eating meat. I guess none of us can face knowing how Emma would feel if we ate something that actually "contains death."

We don't compare letters from Emma, even though we all get them. We don't talk about Emma at all, actually. It's like an unwritten rule.

It's like I really am an only child.

Emma still writes me letters that don't say much. She tells me stories about how nice the nurses are, but she doesn't talk about the other patients, because she says it's all confidential and she's not supposed to. She tells me about what books she reads and what TV shows she's watching. But she doesn't say anything about coming home. When we visit her, she's polite and friendly and tells us she's homesick but fine. She's always fine. It's just another day!

Just another crappy *day,* I think.

Tonight, my dad has made calzones stuffed with four types of cheese, and I've done my usual devour-half-and-start-to-feel-sick routine. My mom picks at her food, as always. She eats it all, but slowly. Painfully slowly. And I decide I really can't take this not-talking-about-Emma game anymore.

"Why hasn't anyone said when Emma's actually coming home?" I ask after forcing myself to drink my milk. "It's almost February break."

My mom and dad exchange a look, as if I'm not sitting here.

"What?" I ask.

My dad finishes chewing and sips his wine.

My mom does the same.

"It's complicated," my dad says.

"Why?"

They do their private-look exchange again. The one where they don't talk but say everything.

"We don't want to worry you," my mom says quietly.

The food in my stomach seems to harden and curdle. "Well, obviously I'm worried even more now," I say.

My mom motions for my dad to be the one to explain.

He reaches out to touch my arm, as if he wants me to hold still while he tells me the news. "The therapy team is concerned about Emma's progress," he says. "She's . . . not quite where they hoped by now."

I feel my food starting to come up my throat, and

force it back down again. "Where they hoped?" I ask. *What does that mean?*

My mom reaches over to touch my hand, but I slide it away. "It's just taking more time than we thought it would," she says. "We have to try to be patient. She's in a safe place. That's what's important."

"So, does she just stay there forever? How are you guys going to pay for this?"

"We're fine."

"No, we aren't! I've heard you fighting about it."

My dad drinks his wine. "Insurance covers a fair amount, and we can get by with the rest. It'll be hard, but we'll be OK."

"Sometimes I really hate her," I say.

"No, you don't," my dad says. "You hate her disease."

"She doesn't have cancer!" I say. "She's the one making herself sick!"

"Stop it!" My mom slams her fork onto the table. "You know it's more complicated than that. She wants to come home, but it's not safe yet. She needs to stay there as long as it takes to get well, no matter what. We're not going to risk losing her."

"Losing her?"

"Louise!" my dad says, shocked.

"She could have *died*, Jeff!" my mom cries. "Let's be honest for a change!"

My dad glares at her. "She's fine. She's going to be fine."

"She didn't *really* almost die," I say. "Did she?"

A whimper comes from under the table. The Captain hates when we fight.

My mom takes another long sip of wine. Her hand is shaking.

My dad gets up from the table and grabs his plate. There's still half a calzone on it. "No," he says, glaring at my mom. "She didn't." But it feels like a lie.

"Where are you going?" my mom asks him.

"I lost my appetite."

"Sit back down."

"I'm not hungry, either," I say.

"You will both sit down and eat what's on your plates. Now."

My dad slowly sits back down.

"I can't eat it," I say. Already the food that formed into a ball feels like it's winding up again and getting ready to shoot out my throat and across the table.

"I said *eat*," my mom says.

You wouldn't say that to Emma, I think.

My dad and I stare at our plates, not eating.

"I'm sorry," my mom says more calmly.

"It's all right," my dad says.

I look up at both of them. At their tired, worn-out faces. So much sadness and disappointment has settled over their eyes, they look like they've aged five years since Christmas.

"It's not all right," I say. "It never will be. Not until Emma comes home."

My mom starts to cry. A tear slips off her chin and lands on her plate, just missing what's left of her calzone. She wipes her face with the cuff of her sweater. It reminds me of something Emma would do.

"What's wrong with you?" my dad asks me. "You could see she was getting upset. Why did you have to make it worse?"

"I'm not the one making things worse! Emma is!"

"It's not Emma — it's the disease."

"But how did she get it? Did we make her sick? What did we do?"

My dad pushes his plate away. "I don't know, Noah. I don't seem to have any answers these days."

My mom cries harder.

Suddenly all the food looks disgusting. I want to shove it off the table.

My mom reaches over and touches my arm. "None of this is your fault, honey," she says. "And you didn't make me cry."

"Yes, I did," I say. "I'm sorry."

"I need to go lie down," she says, which means she needs to go cry harder and she doesn't want me to see.

After she leaves, my dad gets up and hugs me from behind. It feels awkward. "I'm sorry I snapped at you, Noah. I know how hard this is, and I know you need us. I'm sorry if we do a crappy job sometimes."

"It's OK," I say, even though I don't really think it is.

"I'm going to go check on your mom."

The table's a mess, so I take everything into the kitchen, scraping the food into the trash. The Captain wanders in innocently and looks confused when he sees the food in the trash and not in his bowl.

"It's not good for you," I tell him.

I load the dishwasher and wash the other dishes in the sink. Then I go back and wipe the table until everything is clean and perfect. Only it isn't.

I go upstairs and find my letters from Emma. All

the lies about wanting to come home and see me soon and all the other fake things she said to make me feel better. I want to rip them up. I want to take a marker and scribble out all her stupid cartoons. Instead, I run down the hall and into her room and start tearing it apart.

I open drawers in her bureau and go through her stupid clothes, looking for food she might have hidden. That's what all the pamphlets on eating disorders say. How sometimes people hoard food. How they eat it in private and then make themselves throw up. I imagine Emma stuffing her face in here. Did she cry while she did it? Did she laugh, thinking how stupid we were because she was fooling us all?

I look under the bed and find a bunch of shoe boxes, but they're all filled with letters and old papers, not snacks. I'm surprised when I find a box that says NOAH on the top and am scared to open it, but of course I do anyway. Inside, there are all the homemade cards and drawings I've made for her since I was little and learned to hold a crayon. Every single one. It makes my heart hurt so much, it's hard to breathe.

I put the boxes away and then keep looking. I don't even know what I'm looking for, but it doesn't matter.

I search her closet, but it's just stuffed with clothes all hanging neatly on hangers. I check hoodie pockets, but there's nothing there.

I check under her mattress. Nothing.

I try everyplace I can think of, even though I don't even know why I'm looking anymore or what I'll do if I find something.

Finally, I sit on her bed, exhausted.

Emma's room is so much neater than mine, even after my rampage through her stuff. Everything is orderly. Even her posters seem unmarred, where mine have little tears at the corners. She uses that sticky stuff that's like Silly Putty to make them stick to the wall so she doesn't have to use thumbtacks. My walls are covered with thumbtack holes from various posters I've had over the years. Hers are totally perfect. Everything about Emma, as usual, is perfect.

Except for the one thing.

Why can't she be perfect at staying healthy?

Why can't she be perfect at that?

Next to her bed, she has a little nightstand where she keeps her favorite books, including photo books she's made of her friends. But there's also one I don't remember. It says *My Life* on the spine. I pull it out and flip through the pages. Some of the photos I recognize, but a lot I don't remember. She must have gotten them from my mom's computer.

I don't know why she never showed it to me. She's made a bunch of cute captions to go with each spread. There are photos of her trying to teach me how to walk. Feeding me from a bottle. Drawing with me at the kitchen table. Posed photos of us sitting in front of the Christmas tree for our family holiday card.

But as we get older, there are a lot of photos I didn't even realize she had taken. Me, Sam, and Ryan sitting out back in the grass, talking. She must have taken it from her bedroom window. There's a shot of me in the Lewises' carpool, looking miserable. She must have taken it with her phone when I wasn't paying attention. There's a photo of my dad busy cooking in the kitchen, the Captain standing behind him hopefully. There's one of my mom asleep on the couch with an open book resting on her chest. Something called *This Dark Road to Mercy*. I wonder if Emma took the photo because of the book's title or because of my mom.

The next spread shows my bedroom on one side and Emma's on the other. On the next spread, there's a photo of my parents' dresser top covered with framed photos, some that are in this book. I keep flipping, feeling lonelier with each page. The photos went from such happy times to such lonely ones. Photos of objects and rooms, not people, but where people should be. Like the dining-room table, set for dinner but with no one sitting there. Or the living-room couch with a magazine tossed on a cushion.

There's a photo of a box of Christmas ornaments, as if they're waiting to be hung but no one's around to do it.

There's a photo of the outside of our house. The driveway. The car. Our old swing set.

If I were a stranger looking at this book, I would see how the pictures went from warm and filled with love to cold and sad, as if all that filled it up at the beginning had disappeared.

A sad coldness envelops me as I finish the final pages. The last photo is of Emma's closed bedroom door. I turn the page as if I'm opening the door, and I find one more picture, along with a piece of old paper folded small, taped inside the back cover. The photo is of a locker door at school with THE REAL BEAST written on it in thick black letters. I know right away this is Emma's locker and that someone did this to her.

Someone wanted to make her feel bad about her list. I slip the folded paper from the tape and slowly unfold it. THE REAL BEAST, it says, as if whoever wrote on her locker left her a note, too. Only it's not the same writing style from the picture. After reading so many of Emma's letters lately, I know it's her own handwriting. Whoever left the first note convinced her it was true.

I shut the book as my already aching heart squeezes itself into something that hurts so much I have to sit and squeeze my eyes shut just as tightly and wait for the pain to go away.

How long ago did Emma make this book? How did she pay for it? She would have had to ask for my mom's credit card. My mom probably thought it was another friend photo book. But if she saw this, if she saw that closed door, if she saw the note, what would she think?

I wonder if she would feel like I do now. Like the sad cold has made its way inside me, and I'll never feel warm or happy again.

"You're not a beast," I whisper to the empty room. "You never were."

I put the book back on the shelf and get up to leave, making sure I return everything to the way it was. It feels so quiet and still and empty in here. As if Emma's been gone for months. As if she's never coming back.

Instead of closing her door when I leave, I prop it open with the biggest book I can find, *Harry Potter and the Deathly Hallows*. It's the last book we read together. I decide in my next letter I'll ask her if we can read it again when she comes home.

When, or *if*?

When. It has to be when.

I'm trying really hard.

That's what she wrote. She's trying. As long as she's trying, she'll be OK. As long as she doesn't give up.

I step out into the hall and listen for noises downstairs, but the house is quiet. Even the Captain seems to be in hiding.

I'm sure my parents expect me to do my homework and go to bed. When we were little, they would take turns reading to us at bedtime. Emma would come sit on my bed with me, and we'd listen to a few chapters from a book we both agreed on. I always felt like the lucky one because I was snug in my bed and Emma had to get up and go back to hers. She'd wrap herself up in a fuzzy green bathrobe and slippers and bring her pillow in and lie down next to me. Sometimes she fell asleep and stayed with me through the night. But that was when I was really young.

I remember how I loved feeling her warmth next to me. Her quiet, steady breathing made me feel safe.

Now my parents never read to us. They say good night and expect us to go up and take care of ourselves. I don't remember when that started—if one day they simply said, "That's the end of that. You're too old for reading stories to." But I do remember sometimes when Emma was reading a book she really loved, she'd come to my room and ask if she could read to me because she couldn't keep it to herself. She'd read a few pages and stop and want to talk about what was happening. We'd stay up late and argue. One summer we reread the entire Harry Potter series that way, looking for all the clues we'd missed the first time we'd had it read to us by our parents. I bet if I read it now, I'd hear Emma's voice in my head. Her botched attempts at accents. Her cracked voice during the sad parts.

I pick my backpack up off the floor and start to pull out my homework. I have no idea what I have due tomorrow, and I don't think I care. What does it matter?

As I pull out my stuff, my phone slips onto the bed. I don't even know why I bother with it now that no one talks to me. I turn it on anyway and wait to see if I have any messages. I don't, of course. I scan through the photos of Sam and Ryan and me, just to torture myself, I guess. Most of the photos are ridiculous. Ryan peeking over the bathroom stall. Sam making stupid faces at me.

I find a few I didn't know were there. Probably because Ryan took my phone and added a bunch. He thinks that's the funniest thing on earth. There's one of Lily walking away (probably supposed to be her butt). One of Sam's sandwich (a close-up of the meat). One of the inside of Sam's mouth filled with chewed-up food.

A few weeks ago, I would have thought that was gross but funny. Now it just makes me feel sad.

Before I think too much about it, I press CALL on Ryan's name. Then I hang up.

About four seconds later, my phone buzzes.

"Hi," I say.

"Did you butt-dial me or something?" he asks.

"No."

"So you were just calling and hanging up?"

"I don't know. I guess I changed my mind. Sorry."

He's quiet a minute. "So . . . do you want to talk to me or not?"

"I . . . yes."

"OK. What's up?"

"Not much."

The Captain wanders into my room and sniffs the air in a judgey-looking way. As if *he* should talk. I pat my thigh, and he comes over and licks my hand reassuringly, then lies down at my feet.

"Have you heard from Emma?" Ryan asks.

"Yeah. She's not coming home for a while."

"Oh. I'm really sorry she's sick. I . . . Sam and I. We wondered if she was OK—before—but didn't know how to tell you. We noticed she seemed really thin, but . . . we didn't think . . ."

"It's all right," I say.

"She's going to be OK, though. Right?"

"Yeah. I think so. But it's not safe for her to come home yet, so . . ."

"What do you mean?"

I look at my messy posters and the holes in my wall.

"She's still . . . struggling."

"I'm sorry, Noah."

"Thanks."

There's an awkward silence. It feels weird talking again. It's like we lost our rhythm and don't know how to get it back. Like how it feels after being away at summer camp for two weeks and it seems as if so much has changed, even though back home nothing has.

"Are you and Sam still in a fight?" I ask.

"Nah. We made up. He's just annoying, you know? Sometimes his annoying-ness builds up too high, and I have to blow up at him so it can go back to zero again."

I laugh a little. "Yeah."

"So," he says, a little quietly, "I'm kind of dating someone."

"What?"

"Yeah."

"Who?"

"Sasha Finnegan."

"No way!"

"Yeah. I like older women."

I laugh again, this time for real.

"She's actually the one who asked me out. Can you believe that?"

"Wow."

"I know. All the eighth-grade boys hate me now. It's kind of awesome."

"Does this mean you have to stop being an emu?"

"Emo. And yeah. It didn't really suit me, anyway. Acting moody all the time is kind of exhausting."

He fills me in on all the details, and I listen and care. It feels so good to be talking about something positive for a change. Something that's good and new and hopeful.

"I also happen to know that Sadie truly does like you. You know. Because she's friends with Sasha. So. There's that. If you ever want to be normal again and stop being such a loner."

I don't answer.

"You should probably ask her out. She doesn't like to be single, so I don't think your window of opportunity is going to be open very long."

I take a deep breath and lean back on my bed and look up at the ceiling.

"How do I ask her out?" I ask. "Tell me what to do."

"Well, first you have to have the guts to walk up to her," he starts. Then he lists all the tips he knows, which is surprisingly a lot, given that he has only had one girlfriend and only for a few days. Then I promise I'll do it. And just like that, we're friends again.

When we get off the phone, things feel a little more right and a lot less lonely. The coldness I felt earlier doesn't feel so strong. I go to bed without doing my homework. Instead, I go to sleep thinking about how I'm going to ask Sadie Darrow out. For the first time in forever, I sleep straight through the night. I don't dream about Emma calling out and no one hearing. I don't dream about locked bathroom doors and trying to break them down. I don't dream at all. I just sleep. I wake up extra early, but I feel more rested than I have in weeks. I feel ready to go back to school. I feel ready to be me again. And I almost think I know what that means.

Because it's so early, the house is still quiet. I get up and go back to Emma's room. I find the note inside her book and take it back to my room. I begin to re-create the happy images from the book by sketching them, then coloring them in. I add other happy-memory images, like of Emma reading to me, and of Emma holding the Captain as a puppy. And Emma leaning into my bedroom doorway to say good night. Then I

carefully cross out THE REAL and write YOU ARE NOT
A before the word BEAST. I fold it back up and put it in
an envelope. I write down her temporary address on it
and stick it in my backpack. She's not a beast. No one
is. We're all just human, trying to live another day. Just
another day.

22

Instead of a Complaint, Here's a Tip: Seize the Day!

"I heard you're talking to us again," Sam says. He and Ryan are waiting for me outside on the steps. Sam reaches out his hand to shake.

I smack it aside. "Yeah, you dope. But I'm not shaking your hand."

He shoves it into his pocket, all self-conscious.

Ryan nudges him.

"I was just trying to be friendly," Sam says. "What's so wrong with that?"

"Nothing," I say.

"We're just looking out for you, Sam," Ryan adds. "People don't shake hands like that. You're not thirty-five, and this isn't some business meeting."

"Oh."

"Don't worry about it," I say.

Sam shrugs. "Well, I'm glad we're friends again."

"Me too," I say. "Sorry for being a jerk."

"It's understandable," Sam says. "Given the circumstances." He pauses. "Ryan told me you're going to ask Sadie out."

"Yup!" Ryan agrees. "Time to seize the day, Noah!"

"That's great advice," Sam says. "I'm gonna put that in the box."

"But it's not a complaint," I say.

"Well, it's a pretty good suggestion, don't you think?"

I can't argue.

"Here," I say, handing Ryan a folded-up piece of paper.

"What's this?"

"Something I promised you a long time ago."

He unfolds the paper carefully and then smiles when he sees my drawing. I used the photo from

Emma's book to draw the picture of the three of us talking in the grass.

"This is great," Ryan says. "Told you you were a real artist."

"Anyway," I say, letting myself smile a little and turning to Sam, "how are things with Molly? Are you back together?"

"Oh, yeah. That was just a little argument. Things are amazing."

Ryan rolls his eyes, and we all go inside before Sam can say, "What's wrong with things being amazing?"

As we walk toward our lockers, we act like nothing is different. Like it used to be. Like there's not this huge horrible thing happening to my sister. But now I feel less mad about it. Less guilty.

When Curly sees me, she races over and rubs my legs, and I pick her up. She's wearing her Teen-Me doll vest. She purrs like crazy when I hold her against my chest.

"Crazy cat," I say.

She struggles to get down again, but then keeps circling my legs while I put stuff in my locker and get ready for class.

Ryan goes over to Sasha at her locker, and they hold hands. Ryan glances over at me, and I give him a thumbs-up. He smiles and shakes his head. I don't think I've ever seen him look so happy. So *un-emu*.

I glance around for Sadie, just to see if maybe she'll say hi to me or give me some sign that she really likes me. But when I find her, she's with Zach Bray, and he's doing some kind of dance around her, swinging his hips and singing while she laughs. I guess the window of opportunity just closed on my fingers.

During lunch, the Tank comes to find me and asks to see me in his classroom. Instead of a regular lunch bag, he has a small cooler. He opens it and takes out a huge sandwich, a thermos, and a bag of veggie chips. Not a snack size, a full bag.

"Hungry?" I ask.

He pats his chest. "A body needs fuel. You guys wear me out."

I nod.

Curly meanders around the room, sniffing at the heater along the wall.

"Sniffing out mice," the Tank says. "Good girl."

I take my peanut butter and jelly sandwich out of my lunch bag and start eating.

The Tank slides his bag of chips over to me. I prefer kettle-cooked chips. Potato. Oily. "Veggie chips are so weird," I tell him.

"They grow on you," the Tank says, as if he could read my thoughts.

I take a bite of an orange one. "That's what Emma says, but it hasn't happened yet," I say, making a face.

He smiles and takes a handful.

I'm not sure why he invited me here, but I figure he'll tell me eventually. We eat quietly, watching Curly prowl around.

The Tank hands me a cookie. "My wife made these. She made me promise to share with someone who seemed to need one."

"Is that why you asked me to eat lunch with you?"

He nods.

"Thanks," I say.

"You got it."

I take a bite. Chocolate chip and raisin. I could do without the raisins, but it's still pretty good.

"So, Noah," he says, eating half his cookie in one bite, "how are you holding up?"

I shrug. "I'm OK."

"Any news from Emma?"

I guess this is going to be the question I have to figure out how to answer until Emma comes home, whenever that will be. *When.*

I shrug again. "We see her on weekends. She's getting better."

"That's good to hear. You must be pretty worried about her."

"Yeah."

I finish my cookie. It's hard to swallow the last bite. The usual tightness in my stomach starts to grow and crawl up my throat.

"I wish it wasn't taking so long," I tell him.

He nods and glances toward the window. It's a sunny winter day. The snow is bright and the sunlight sparkles off the snowbanks.

"It's a horrible thing," he says. "Terrible."

"She's still not really herself," I say. "It's like, in losing all that weight, she also lost who she really is. I feel like I don't know her. Like Emma is gone, and there's this stranger living in her body. It's like . . ." I swallow the hurt rising up in my throat.

"It's like she died," I say quietly. "Or at least part of her died."

The Tank reaches over and squeezes my shoulder. "I'm so sorry," he says. "I've taught here a lotta years, and I've seen kids struggle with stuff like this over and over. Eating disorders. Cutting. Drugs, too. Sometimes when we teachers learn about it, we're shocked. We had no idea the kid was feeling bad inside. Depression is a strange thing, and it manifests in all kinds of ways. We try to help, but sometimes kids need more than us. They need specialists who understand how these things work. It's good your parents sent Emma to a place where people really understand what she's going through."

"But she never seemed depressed," I say. "Why did she get depressed?"

"I don't know, Noah. Sometimes there's no logical reason. Sometimes it can be a chemical thing in the brain."

"Really?" I think about the BEAST note and wonder if that could be true. If she got sick because of something in her brain, or because she wanted to punish herself. I remember all the sad photos in that book.

The ones without people in them. Only objects. And I just don't know. I don't know what to think anymore.

"Emma is in a safe place," the Tank says. "Knowing you support her and love her is the best thing you can do to help her. Send her letters. Let her know you're thinking of her."

"I do."

"That's real good."

We eat some more cookies, and the Tank goes over to his desk and opens a drawer.

"Here," he says. "I saved this for you. I had a feeling you might want it back."

He holds out the Emma sculpture. She's distorted and misshapen, and the face is all smooth where Curly licked it blank.

"Thanks," I say. I take it and get my stuff.

"You should finish that," the Tank says. "Or make another."

"Yeah," I say. "Maybe." But part of me thinks it makes sense to leave her unfinished, blank face and all. Only Emma can reshape who she wants to be.

I leave him and wander over to the art room. It's still lunch period, so the halls are mostly empty, though I can hear laughter coming from the Community Room.

I don't bother to turn on the lights in the art room. There's sunlight pouring through the windows, casting dusty beams across the clean work surfaces. I get one of the new sculptures I've been working on and bring it over to a table.

"Hey! There you are!" Sam and Ryan come bounding into the room, followed by Sasha and Molly.

"We were looking for you!" Sam says.

"What are you doing in here?" Sasha asks, coming closer. "Oh! Is that your new sculpture project? Let's see!"

"I'm not finished," I say.

They all gather around to inspect.

"Jeez, Noah. You really are a good artist," Sam says. "What is it?"

I shrug, embarrassed to tell them. I look down at the forms rising out of the clay. Four heads and necks, all touching and connected. My family. I've been working on it for a while now but can't seem to figure out how to finish it.

Molly puts her arm around Sam. They look natural together. Like they've been together forever. I think if a girl did that to me, I'd melt to the floor. I guess Sam isn't as goofy as I thought.

Ryan and Sasha are holding hands again. Ryan doesn't look nearly as comfortable doing this as Sam does, which I plan to point out later, just to make sure he doesn't get too full of himself. These two can't let their relationship status go to their heads.

"Noah, are you ever going to ask Sadie out?" Sasha asks. "I really think she likes you."

"Yeah, Noah! You have to ask her!" Sam says like an excited little kid. "Remember, you better seize the day, because she doesn't like to be single."

"I'm not really ready for a committed relationship right now," I say.

Ryan rolls his eyes.

"Plus, she was dancing with Zach earlier. I think they might be a thing."

"I told you not to wait!" Ryan slaps his forehead with his free hand. "At least she didn't go for Max."

"What's wrong with Max?" Molly asks.

Ryan and I hold out our muscle-less arms at the same time and mimic how he moves.

"What's wrong with your arms?" Sam asks.

Ryan laughs.

Then I laugh.

Then we're all laughing, even though I'm not sure

anyone actually knows why. It's a relief laugh. I can tell. We're all relieved to be laughing together again. It doesn't matter why.

"I need to work on this," I say. "But I'll see you guys later."

"Yeah, sure," Ryan says. "C'mon, guys, let's leave the artist in peace."

They leave me alone again, but I don't feel lonely.

I reorganize Emma's tools, then prep my sculpture, wetting the cracks and smoothing out the curves. I think about what kind of glaze I'll use when I fire it. Or maybe I won't use any glaze at all. I'm not sure.

All I know is that when I'm done, I'm going to leave it on Emma's desk in her room as a welcome-home gift. I think she'll like that. I think she'll like knowing that I was thinking of her while she was away, working on something special for her. And that I knew, that I really believed, that she'd get well again and come back home to receive it.

But for now, it's still a work in progress. Just like Emma. Just like me, I guess. Just like my family. And that's all right. For the first time in a long time, I feel like everything really will be OK. Today is just another day. And it finally feels like a good one.

Acknowledgments

Many people assume that writing a book is a solitary endeavor, but I've been extremely fortunate to have the company of Cindy Faughnan and Debbi Michiko Florence, my virtual office mates, since this journey began. Thank you, dear WWaWWas, for your love and support, and for your invaluable comments and suggestions. Thanks also to my agent, Barry Goldblatt, for your continued guidance, and to my husband, Peter Carini, for your honest feedback and encouragement. Extra special thanks to my editor, Joan Powers, who gives me the courage to dig a little deeper with every revision, and who always helps me have faith that the longer, harder road will be worth taking. Joan, I am so grateful to call you my editor. And finally, a huge thank-you to my son, Eli Carini, who shared many of the original Suggestion Box entries that found their way into this book as we carpooled home from school. Eli, thank you for sharing your input, your humor, and your heart. You inspire me every day.